Bridesmaid

of

Honor

Graysen Morgen

2013

Bridesmaid of Honor © 2013 Graysen Morgen

Triplicity Publishing, LLC

ISBN-13: 978-0988619647

ISBN-10: 0988619644

Printed in the United States of America

First Edition – 2013

Cover Design: Triplicity Publishing, LLC

Interior Design: Triplicity Publishing, LLC

Also by Graysen Morgen

Acknowledgements

Special thanks to CJ, my eagle eyes down under! Also, thank you to Carol, my newest beta reader. You both worked hard pointing out all of the common mistakes that I repeatedly made.

Multas gratias!

Dedication

This book is dedicated to my partner. If you hadn't come to me one afternoon with a crazy story about a co-worker that made me laugh, this book would never have been written.

ani ohevet otach

Chapter One

The gunmetal gray Porsche Cayman sports car careened into a parking space, skidding to a stop. The door swung open and the driver slid out wearing a dark, form-fitting pantsuit with an off-white blouse cut daringly low, almost making it appear as if there was nothing under her jacket. She closed the door, turning towards the restaurant as her long chestnut hair blew in loose waves around her shoulders in the breeze. The dark stilettos on her feet clicked a steady cadence as she walked across the parking lot.

Heather Young sat at a small table in the corner sipping a light-bodied glass of wine, watching her best friend since childhood as she walked towards the restaurant. Heather admired her friend's natural beauty. She exuded sex appeal and looked like she belonged on magazine covers, but anyone who knew her knew that was the last thing she would ever want to do. No, Britton Prescott was definitely not a model or actress. Tucked away behind the fashionable pantsuit hugging her lithe figure, was the body of an athlete and the mind of an artist who would much rather be wearing an old pair of

1

jeans and a worn T-shirt than the Armani suit. Heather watched as Britton pushed her Oakley sunglasses up on her head when she entered the restaurant. She waved in her direction when she saw her looking around.

"I'm sorry I'm late. I got stuck in traffic downtown. I think the tourist season is starting early this year. It's barely spring," Britton said, slipping into the seat across from Heather. "Wine?" she questioned with a raised eyebrow. "Are you not going back to work today?"

"Nope. It's Friday. Did you forget the dental office closes early on Fridays?" Heather asked, tucking her long, strawberry blond hair behind her ear. "Besides, I'm ready to pull my hair out over the wedding. I'm beginning to think Greg and I should elope. Maybe we can all just go to Vegas for the weekend or something."

Britton laughed. "Your mother would have a stroke."

Heather rolled her eyes. "True, but it's my step-monster I want to get rid of."

The waiter walked up to their table, spending way too much time eyeing Britton's cleavage as he took their lunch order.

"Would you care for a glass of wine as well? Or perhaps a dirty martini?" he asked with a grin.

Heather started laughing and choked on the sip of wine she had just swallowed.

"No, thank you," Britton said, "I'd like a glass of water with a lemon."

"That was the worst pickup line I've ever heard," Heather said, shaking her head when he walked away.

"I've heard worse," Britton sighed.

"It must be hard to walk, with all of the men and women throwing themselves at your feet," Heather teased.

"Oh please. If that were true I wouldn't be single again," Britton said, rolling her eyes as she picked up the menu. "Anyway, what has the old battle-axe done now?" Britton knew Heather couldn't stand her stepmother and she often had to compete with her for her father's attention since her parent's divorce her freshman year of college.

"Wait, what happened to Victoria? I thought that was back on again?" Heather asked.

"It's off for good. I'm starting to think she's a little crazy."

"A little?"

Britton laughed and shrugged. "She's good in bed."

"So, that's a reason to keep her around?"

"Why not? I don't see the people lined up at my feet that you seem to think are there," Britton said.

Heather shook her head.

"So, what did Marianne do to ruffle your feathers this time?"

Heather huffed. "She thinks her daughter's going to be a bridesmaid in my wedding."

"Leslie?"

"Yes."

"You don't even talk to her."

"Exactly!"

"What did your mom say?"

"She called my dad and told him she planned the wedding with only one bridesmaid since Greg only has a best man and one groomsman and there was no room for Leslie. His response was basically, he is paying for it so Leslie will be a bridesmaid and she needs to figure it out. I swear, since the divorce they've become so aggressive with each other. It's like two boxers who trade jabs every chance they get, with me in the middle."

"That's ridiculous. What are you going to do? Wait, who is the bridesmaid? I thought you and Greg decided on just the maid of honor and best man?"

"That's why I called you to meet me for lunch," Heather paused when Britton's cell phone rang.

Britton checked her phone and sent the call to her voicemail. "It's Bridget. I'll call her back later. My mother is driving her crazy with her wedding planning too. I think they're changing the date again or something."

"I can't believe your sister and I are both getting married."

"Yeah, me neither. That's way too much wedded bliss for me," Britton scoffed. Getting married was the farthest thing from her mind and something she didn't really want anyway, but when her best friend asked her to be her maid of honor and her sister asked her to be a bridesmaid, she couldn't refuse either one.

"So, the bridesmaid is going to be my cousin Daphne," Heather said. She held her breath, watching her best friend's face distort as the words entered her mind.

"Excuse me?! Daphne the bitch we can't stand? How the fuck did she weasel her way into your wedding party?" Britton spat.

"She's my only cousin and my mom thought it would be a good idea."

"Well, put your foot down and tell her no."

"She's changed a lot since high school, Britt."

"Uh-huh, sure she has. She made my life a living hell in high school." Britton suddenly wished she'd ordered something with alcohol in it. The glass of water sitting in front of her would do nothing to ease the tension in her head.

"She doesn't even live here anymore," Heather said.

"What do you mean? I thought she was still working for my family."

"She's still at Prescott's, but she got promoted a year or two ago. Her office is at the distribution center up in New Bedford. I haven't seen her recently. She rarely comes home."

"I had no idea. I mean I knew dad was expanding the company out of Rhode Island and had opened stores up in Massachusetts, but I didn't realize it was enough for a separate DC.

"That's because you refuse to know anything about the huge grocery company your family owns and operates. Hell, your family employs thirty-percent of the state."

"You're right. I guess I just don't care. I know I'm the black sheep and probably the first Prescott in a hundred years who doesn't work for the company. I just like being an architect a hell of a lot more. I don't like how you changed the subject by the way."

"What?" Heather grinned.

"You know what," Britton sneered.

Heather sighed. "You're my best friend, Britton. Just deal with her, please, for me."

Britton saw the sincerity in her friend's brown eyes. She hated Daphne Atwood and could go the rest of her life without seeing her or hearing her name, but she would do this for Heather.

"If she thinks she's calling the shots on your bachelorette party or bridal shower, I'm going to scratch her eyes out," Britton said, pushing her salad away. She'd lost her appetite.

Heather smiled, knowing damn good and well that Britton would love to kick Daphne's ass after the hell she and Britton's older sister Bridget had put them through in high school. They were a year younger and often forced by Bridget and Britton's parents to tag along with the two older girls who were also best friends. Daphne seemed to blame it all on Britton, causing a huge rift between the two. Things got much worse when Britton and Heather made the school rowing team their freshman year. Britton quickly stood out from the other girls and became the first freshman captain in school history.

Rowing had actually been Britton's whole world. She worked very hard to be the standout star that she was, which was why the entire state was shocked when she turned down multiple rowing scholarships and possible Olympic chances to go to Massachusetts Institute of Technology, one of the hardest design schools in the country to even get into. She wanted to become an architect. Her father was the most disappointed. He and Britton were very close and he always expected her to take his place as the President of the company one day and she showed absolutely no interest. He was still heartbroken when she graduated with her master's degree from MIT a year ago, making the Dean's List each of her six years at the school.

"What's wrong?" Britton asked.

Heather smiled again. "I was just thinking about the past few years. So much has happened since high school. I'm getting married in a few weeks."

"Maybe you should elope, now that I think about it."

Heather raised an eyebrow. "Why is that?"

"We wouldn't have to deal with Daphne or Leslie." She smiled brightly.

Heather shook her head laughing. "That would be too easy."

Britton checked the time on her wristwatch. "I need to get back to the office. I'll call you later," she said, standing and hugging her friend before leaving.

As soon as she pulled out of the parking lot in her car, Britton played the voicemail from her sister.

Britt, it's me. Mom decided not to deal with the country club since their next open date is in September and Wade and I really wanted to get married in the spring. So now the wedding is going to be at the family house in Newport on March 16th. I know that is the weekend before Heather's wedding and only five weeks away, but it should be fine. The invitations went out this morning. Daphne's going to be my maid of honor and you're going to be a bridesmaid. Call me later so we can all figure out a time to go dress shopping, maybe this weekend or something.

"Seriously?! Are you fucking kidding me?!" Britton screamed and threw her cell phone into the passenger floorboard of her car as she careened out of the parking lot.

Chapter Two

The rest of Britton's day went by in a blur. She was glad she didn't have any deadlines hovering over her head because the only thing she could think about was Daphne Atwood. She knew Daphne would be involved with her sister's wedding, they were best friends. However, she did not expect the wedding to be back to back with Heather's, nor had she expected the bombshell Heather dropped on her at lunch with Daphne being in her bridal party. Now, she would have to spend more days in the company of Daphne Atwood than she ever wanted for the rest of her life, and all in the span of a few weeks.

Britton decided as soon as she pulled her complex that she wasn't going to the gym. She walked into her apartment and poured herself a glass of wine before going to her bedroom down the hall. She took a few sips of the cabernet and set the glass on top of her dark cherry dresser that matched the queen-sized sleigh bed and night stands. Her bedroom set was the only thing she had splurged on. The rest of her apartment was modestly decorated with a small coffee colored couch, two brown end tables, and a flat screen TV with a brown, modern-looking entertainment shelf under it. The brown dining table doubled as a home office and was full of drawings and small models.

When she had graduated from college, she moved to Providence to take a temporary position with a local architectural firm versus an unpaid internship at a large corporation on the other side of the country. Her father wasn't pleased with her career choice, but he hadn't cut her off. She still inherited her trust fund after graduation. She treated herself to a brand new sports car since she'd worked her ass off for six years in school. Then she had blown her father's mind when she moved into an apartment in an upscale gated community. He constantly reminded her that she needed to buy and not rent, but she wasn't ready to be tied down to anything and as an architect she dreamed of living in a place she designed from the ground up. Her current job was only temporary for a year and after that she could possibly get a regular position with the firm or find herself unemployed if they decided not to keep her at the end of the temporary contract. The money wasn't really a factor, but her trust fund paid her only so much and since she wasn't an employee of the company her family owned, she was left out to dry and forced to support herself with her chosen career choice.

Britton peeled her suit off, tossing it into the dry clean pile on the floor of her walk-in closet. She picked her heels up and put them on the shelf with the rest of her shoes. She hated wearing high heels, but the men she worked for were old school and expected the women in the office to be dressed to impress the clients and potential clients. She slipped into a pair of soft black cotton shorts that were dangerously short and a green tank top that stretched the word Army across her round breasts. Then she pulled her wavy hair back in a ponytail, revealing two small gold hoops in each of her ears. After removing the earrings, she walked into the bathroom and washed her face. Her natural olive complexion allowed her to go makeup free. She looked at the gray eyes staring back at her and smiled, thinking back to the time when she was a kid and asked her mom when she could start wearing makeup too. Her mother simply told her that she was blessed with natural beauty and would never need to fake her appearance.

Britton finished her glass of wine as she walked back to the living room and stopped in the kitchen to pour another one. She had barely gotten comfortable on the couch when her cell phone rang. She checked the caller ID before answering it. All she really wanted to do was relax and force her mind to think of something else.

"I just heard the news," Heather said.

"What news?" Britton asked, taking an extra sip of wine. Her second glass was almost empty. If she wasn't careful she would swim right to the bottom of the bottle.

"Your sister moving her wedding date to the weekend before mine. I had a feeling Daphne would be Bridget's maid of honor. They've been friends almost as long as we have."

"Yeah, Daphne all month long. Oh what fun," Britton said sarcastically.

"Don't worry about it. I'm sure it will go by quickly. What made her change it to your family home? I thought it was a huge deal to have it at the country club."

"I don't know. I haven't been privy to the planning. My family isn't very religious and neither is Wade's so I figured it wouldn't be in a church."

"My family is no more religious than yours, but my mother insists that the service be held in a church. I don't know. I give up on the whole damn thing," Heather said.

"Yeah, what a mess. I have so much shit on my plate right now. The timing for all of this couldn't be worse for me. My dad's expecting to see the preliminary sketches for the new corporate office building and I know he's going to shoot them down."

"What makes you think that? Didn't he ask you to design a new building for the company?"

"Yes, but you have to think about how he operates. This is a test. If I can't do this then it will prove I am wasting my time trying to be an architect."

"I know he's hard on you, Britt, but you're a strong woman and damn good at what you do. Blow him out of the water and he will realize you're doing what you are meant to be doing. He has to learn to be proud of who you are now, not who he wanted you to be. At least your mother isn't married to a guy close to your age and your father isn't married to a bitch who is jealous of you."

"That's true," Britton laughed. "I keep waiting for your parents to come to their senses."

"Yeah, me too, but don't hold your breath." Heather paused. "So, I'm really sorry about the whole Daphne thing. I wasn't expecting Bridget to change her plans. I would've said no when my mom added her in my bridal party. I know you and Daphne are like oil and water, but she really is different. I talked to her earlier. She's the one who told me about Bridget's change of plans."

Britton knew better. The water between her and Daphne was way too wide to build a bridge over. "I'll believe it when I see it and I'm guessing now I will have plenty of time for that," she said, stretching her legs out and crossing her ankles with her feet on the small ottoman that matched her couch.

When she hung up the phone, Britton decided to forgo the third glass of wine and work on her father's sketches instead, but her mind kept drifting back to all of the wedding hoopla. She needed to get to work planning Heather's bachelorette party and bridal shower. She knew Daphne would be doing the same for Bridget as her maid of honor. They would need to cooperate with each other so that the parties didn't overlap because both weddings and parties would have some of the same guests.

Britton's mind finally settled on the task at hand and she went to work putting the finishing touches on the sketches of the three-story building. Her cell phone rang an hour later, dragging her back to reality. She often lost herself in her designs and loved the feeling of being swept away to another dimension of her mind.

She sighed and flopped down on the couch as she answered the call.

"Isn't it a little late to be calling me?" Britton said.

"Oh please, you're a night owl and it's Friday night. Tell Victoria to give you a few minutes to talk to your sister since you neglected to call me back this afternoon," Bridget chided.

Britton rolled her eyes, contemplating that third glass of wine. "I got your message. I was busy with work. I'm going out to the house in Newport tomorrow to go over the preliminary drawings of the new building with daddy and I needed to do some last minute work on them."

"That's great. Daphne and I will be there too, going over the wedding plans with mom. You and Daphne can get together to talk about your party planning."

"Oh, isn't that just wonderful," Britton said sarcastically.

"Britt, you need to grow up. High school is over."

"I know she's your best friend, but she's a colossal bitch. What the hell made you change the date, by the way? As if I don't have enough on my plate with Heather's wedding the weekend after. Daphne's in that wedding too, in case you didn't already know. It seems I won't be able to escape her claws like I originally planned."

"You really need to get over your issues with her. We're all adults now."

"Uh-huh. You better tell her that. She's the one who acts like I'm the scum of the earth."

"Damn it, Britton, I didn't call to hear you whine and complain about Daphne. She's my maid of honor and Heather's bridesmaid so you're just going to have to put your big girl pants on and suck it up. Where's Victoria? She should be the one you're bitching to, not me."

"That's old news."

"Oh really?"

"Yes. For good this time. Anyway, why all of the changes all of a sudden?"

Bridget sighed. "Mom got into it with someone at the country club a few days ago when they told her our guest list was over their capacity for the reception room we rented. The larger room they're building will not be ready until September. She doesn't want to cut anyone from the list, so everything got moved to the house in Newport. That's where mom and daddy were married anyway."

13

Britton couldn't think of a reason not to have the wedding at the family home. It was a huge estate that had been in the family for nearly a decade and reminded Britton of the Kennedy estate on Cape Cod. The grounds were close to a hundred acres of sprawling hills that rolled down to a cliff that overlooked the Atlantic Ocean with a small pathway that snaked through the rocks down to a private beach area that was hidden during high tide. The house itself was two stories with six bedrooms, two family rooms, a large industrial kitchen, and five bathrooms. It had started as a small two bedroom house with a single bathroom and over the years, as each generation took over the property, the house grew. Britton and Bridget's grandfather, Dewey Prescott, was the last person to have the home upgraded. He'd had the kitchen redone, two bedrooms, another bathroom, and a pool added.

"I think it's a beautiful place to get married, Bridget. I just don't like that it's back to back with Heather's wedding."

"I know, but that's the only date we could do it. The tent rental place had a cancellation for that weekend. Otherwise, we would have had to wait until June. I talked to Daphne and she said Heather didn't mind."

No, she wouldn't because she will be too busy with her own wedding and Daphne's not as much of a bitch to her as she is to me and she's not in both weddings! Britton thought.

"I'll see you in the morning and please behave, Britton. High school is over. Daphne's looking forward to seeing you," Bridget said before hanging up.

"Oh I'm sure she is," Britton growled, tossing the phone to the other end of the couch.

Chapter Three

"This isn't exactly what I was hoping to see, Britton," her father said. He was sitting behind his desk in the study of the large estate house.

Britton looked around at the ornate walls decorated with awards from the state and pictures of the company over the last decade. She always felt small in this room, even when she had visited her grandparents at the family house and her grandfather would be sitting in the same seat her father sat in. Dewey Prescott was a hard man, but he held a soft spot for Britton and often snuck her grandmother's cookies into the office for them to share. Her father, Stephen Prescott, was equally as hard as his father had been and carried the same soft spot for Britton, at least he did until the day she told him she was going to MIT to be an architectural designer. She knew she broke his heart when she told him the family business didn't interest her and she disappointed him when she gave up rowing to draw and play with models. He had always told her the open space behind his desk was where he was going to hang her Olympic gold medal one day.

Britton straightened her posture in the chair across from him and ran her hands over the dark slacks covering her thighs. She was dressed business casual in dark slacks, a white button down blouse with three-quarter sleeves pushed back and a wide open collar. She wore black, slip-on loafers and kept her wavy hair down around her shoulders, the chestnut color shining brightly in the mid-morning sun filtering in through the windowpanes. She wasn't big on wearing jewelry, so she had just a small watch on with a thin gold band, and both pairs of her small gold hoop earrings.

"What would you like changed, daddy?" she asked. This was the first time she'd actually drawn or designed anything for him and she was nervous. His opinion intimidated the hell out of her. She was daddy's girl after all and had disappointed him so many times over the last few years. She wondered if she'd ever be able to turn their relationship around.

He pursed his lips in thought. She took the time to look at her dad. She hadn't seen him much since her job kept her so busy. Stephen Prescott was in his fifties and stood just below six feet. He wasn't slender, but he wasn't overweight either. She shared his gray eyes and natural olive complexion, but his brown hair had turned gray and was on the verge of going completely white in the near future. He was wearing a dark blue oxford shirt with the sleeves rolled back and tan trousers with brown loafers. He used to enjoy the occasional cigar, but after his father had died of lung cancer, he quit partaking in the delight of a smoke and a glass of brandy, a trait he'd learned from his father.

He pushed the drawings aside and put his elbows on the desk with his hands up, forming a triangular point under his chin.

"When I gave you the requirements, I asked for a three-story building with break rooms and restrooms, with various offices on each floor. What are all of these additional rooms? Is this something you would present as a proposal to a client?"

Britton felt her chest tighten. "I changed the conference rooms a little bit and added a media room. I also changed the layout, giving you a corner office with a view and the cubicles on the first floor are for the store operations staff. You used to always say they needed offices together instead of working out of backrooms at stores. I can change it back if you'd like," she said.

She was beginning to wonder if she should be the one handling the design in the first place. Her father didn't like what she was doing with her life and this was his way of shooting it down.

"I like the idea of the cubicles. I don't need a corner office with a view and we don't need a media room."

"Okay, may I?" she asked, reaching for the interior sketches. She grabbed a pencil from her briefcase and erased a few areas and redrew lines and shading to create different spaces and elements for the top floor offices.

Stephen watched her change the interior lines.

"Is this more like what you're thinking for your office?" she asked, presenting him with an end of the hall room that looked more like an oval office instead of a corner office. Since it was on the interior side it no longer had windows.

He nodded.

Britton took the papers for the middle floor and did the same thing as before, erasing the media room and redrawing the lines for the conference rooms and file rooms.

Britton straightened her back and handed the pages back to him. "This is exactly what you asked for, daddy, and yes, I would be happy to present these to any client."

He wasn't sure what to say to her. "What's the next step?"

"You initial each page and I turn them into a 3D model. When you approve the model, we arrange all of the permits and break ground on your building," she said.

The ball was in her court now and she knew it. She had given him exactly what he wanted and he no longer had any ground to stand on. She watched as he initialed each page and slid the pile back over to her side of the desk.

"I'll start your model on Monday. It can take anywhere from two weeks to a month to build the model. Once it's complete, you and I can meet again to go over it."

"That's fine. I look forward to seeing it, Britton. I have to admit, I'm a little intrigued by all of this. It will be interesting to see what the model looks like, as long as you don't go overboard with your ideas. This is supposed to be a simple corporate office. Remember that. "

~

Britton was glad to be finished with her father's scrutinizing and knew she couldn't leave without seeing her mother. She walked around the house until she heard voices coming from the solarium.

"Hello, Sweetheart," her mother said when Britton walked through the doors.

Sharon Prescott stood up and walked over to her youngest daughter. She could easily pass as a twin or movie double for Diane Keaton. They had the same shaggy haircut with multiple high and lowlights, brown eyes and high cheek bones. They even dressed similarly. Sharon was wearing dark brown slacks and a cream colored blouse.

"Hi, mom," Britton said, giving her a hug.

"You look tired. How did it go with daddy?"

"He's a stubborn man, but I think it went well. I just wanted to say hi. I'm heading back to Providence. I have a lot of work to do."

"At least sit and eat something before you go. I never get to see you as it is." Sharon ushered her daughter over to the table full of brunch food.

"Hey, Britt," Bridget said, walking into the room.

Britton looked up at her sister, but her eyes immediately went to the woman behind her. She had short blond hair, cut in a long bob style and tucked behind her ears and a slender, lithe figure. Britton's eyes roamed over the stranger languidly, stopping when her eyes locked on light green ones staring daggers back at her under a raised eyebrow. Britton swallowed the lump in her throat, tamping down her racing libido. She never noticed her mother leave the room.

"I was just leaving," Britton said.

"Wait, you and Daphne need to get together with your plans before you go," Bridget said.

"I haven't really planned anything yet," Britton said.

"That figures," Daphne smirked sarcastically.

"I'm sure you have everything all planned out. Just give me your damn dates so we can move on," Britton grabbed one of the mimosas her mother had on the table, emptying it in one long sip. She was already on edge from dealing with her father and his constant changes to her designs. Seeing Daphne for the first time in years, only to notice her body's sudden appeal, added fuel to the fire.

"I can't believe Heather left you to handle things for her," Daphne said, shaking her head. "Yes, as a matter of fact I do have everything planned for your sister's parties. That's what a maid of honor does. Or did you not know that?"

"Do you see this?" Britton said to Bridget. "And you think I'm the one with issues." *There is no way I'm attracted to her. So what if she's beautiful. She's a bitch!*

"What the hell is with the two of you?" Bridget said.

"Ask Daphne!" Britton said before storming out of the house.

~

Daphne walked through the house to get some air and clear her head. Seeing Britton stirred emotions she thought were long gone. Stopping near the window in the living room, she watched Britton's hair blowing around her shoulders in loose waves as she walked over to a dark gray sports car, disappearing inside. She shivered, thinking of the interest she saw in Britton's gray eyes as they roamed over her body like the touch of a lover.

Chapter Four

The next day, Britton flopped down on the couch with her cell phone in her hand. She didn't want to talk to Daphne, much less ever see her again, but she needed to get Heather's parties planned. She dialed a number and kicked her feet up on the table.

"Mom was pissed when you left yesterday. She was hoping you would stay for dinner," Bridget said, answering the phone.

"She'll get over it. I had things to do. Speaking of, I need to get these damn parties planned and out of my way. Do you have Daphne's number?" Britton asked.

"Yeah," Bridget quickly gave her the number. "I wish you two would figure out whatever the hell is going on between you. High school is over and you're both adults."

"Yeah, well tell your friend that. I'll talk to you later," Britton said, hanging up.

She dialed the number her sister had given her and stared at the phone without hitting the call button.

"This is stupid," she said to herself. Smiling, she erased the number and opened a new text message, inputting the number again before typing.

This is Britton Prescott. I need the dates you have for Bridget's bachelorette party and bridal shower.

She finished the text and hit send. A minute later, her phone chimed, signaling she had a message. She quickly checked the inbox.

It's about time you started planning something. I want to be involved in the plans since Heather's my cousin and I'm in the wedding anyway.

"Oh god damn! Just give me the dates already!" Britton yelled at her phone and began typing again.

Bridget's my sister and you didn't include me in your plans for her parties. Just give me the damn dates or I will plan without them.

Britton hit send. It was barely ten o'clock in the morning and she wanted a drink. "This woman is going to make me become a raging alcoholic!"

You don't have to be an ass. Her bach party and bridal shower are both on the 9th. I think you should plan Heather's bach party and shower for the 1st or 8th.

Britton wrote down the date for the planned parties and quickly typed a final message.

You will see what the days are when you get the damn invitations in the mail.

After that, Britton spent the rest of the day booking a venue and a caterer for Heather's bridal shower, as well as a limo for the bachelorette party, along with making dinner reservations. She also ordered the invitations for both parties online and had them rush delivered. She refused to let her mind drift back to Daphne.

Monday was a longer work day than she had anticipated. She still needed to start the 3D model for her father's building, but she kicked her feet up on the table and drank a glass of wine instead. When her phone rang she figured it was probably Heather, so she answered without checking the caller ID.

"Hey, babe," Britton said with a yawn.

"Hey yourself," Victoria's sultry voice sent chills up her spine.

Britton swallow a sip of wine, changing her tone. "Victoria. I thought you were someone else."

"Dating again already? You do move fast."

"No, as a matter of fact, I thought you were Heather. I'm expecting her call."

"You sound tired."

"Maybe I am. What is it that you want?" Britton answered honestly. She didn't hate her ex, she was just sick of the up and down rollercoaster ride.

"You, of course."

"Well, that's not happening."

Victoria laughed deeply. "Let's have dinner Wednesday night."

"What for?'

"To catch up, say hi. I haven't talked to you in over a month. We can at least be friends, Britt."

"I'm really busy with work and everything else this week."

"Good, all the more reason to break away for a nice quiet dinner and a glass of wine with me."

Britton's mind flashed back on Daphne standing in her parent's solarium. The woman was driving her crazy.

"Fine. Get us a reservation for seven at Leonardo's," Britton said.

"Great," Victoria replied. "I'm looking forward to it."

Britton tossed the phone onto the couch next to her. She was playing with fire, but she wasn't about to get burned. She wasn't interested in getting involved with Victoria again. Three times was three times too many already. She did enjoy casual conversation with her, however.

~

Over the next two days, Britton worked vigorously on her father's model. She hadn't been happy when he asked her to have it finished in the next two weeks. She tried to explain that something like this usually took a month to prepare, not two and a half weeks, but he demanded to see it in two weeks. She wondered if he was pushing her to fail.

It was after six when Britton finally left her office. She rushed through town to the upscale restaurant, arriving at the valet booth with two minutes to spare. Victoria was already inside, standing near the bar, half turned away from the door. Her long, dark hair was neatly twisted up in a tight bun, with small diamonds glistening from her ears. Britton didn't recognize the dark purple dress she was wearing. It was short and sexy, with spaghetti straps and a small slit up the side. Victoria was obviously dressed to impress.

"I'm sorry. I got tied up at the office," Britton said.

Victoria smiled. The bar lights twinkled in her dark brown eyes. "I expected you to be late," she said.

The hostess showed them to a small table in the middle of the room. Neither of them noticed the two blondes sitting a few tables away.

~

"I can't believe it's only a few weeks away. You'll be Mrs. Nipper before you know it," Daphne said.

"I know," Bridget laughed. "I wish I could keep my name."

"That's starting to become more and more common these days."

"Yeah, I know. I'm not very fond of Nipper, but I love Wade. I'll get used to the name."

"Hey, isn't that Britton?" Daphne said, signing the credit card slip for her dinner bill.

Bridget craned her neck to see where Daphne was looking. "Yeah," she said, finishing her glass of wine.

25

"Who's the woman with her?"

"That's Victoria, her ex-girlfriend, or at least I thought she was," Bridget said.

"She looks like a bitch. How long have they been together?" Daphne asked.

"I guess they dated off and on for probably two or three years. She's crazy."

Daphne laughed.

"I'm serious. She goes through these stages of highs and lows. Britton said it's like riding a rollercoaster."

"Weird. What does she do?"

"She's a curator at the art gallery downtown."

"Well, there you go. People that into art are usually a little out there to begin with."

Bridget grabbed her purse. "Let's go say hi," she said.

~

"Do you want to share a bottle of wine?" Victoria asked.

"I probably shouldn't. I still have more work to do when I get home," Britton said, opening the menu. "I think I'll just have a glass."

"What's this big project that has you all tied up?"

"My father asked me to design a new corporate office building for the company. I've been back and forth with him a lot over the past few weeks and now I'm finally putting the model together."

"I thought your father didn't want anything to do with your career?"

"He doesn't, but he asked me to do this, so I'm doing it," Britton paused to order a glass of merlot from the waiter. "Bridget's getting married in a few weeks. I'm a bridesmaid, so I have that going on, as well."

"Isn't Heather getting married soon, too?"

"Yeah," Britton laughed. "Their weddings are a week apart."

"That's crazy. No wonder you're a mess. I know you hate the idea of getting married," Victoria said.

"Yeah, it hasn't been exactly fun. So, how's life at the gallery?"

"It's fine. We're getting a new section devoted to Rembrandt. I've been busy getting that ready."

"Hello, ladies," Bridget said. "Victoria, it's nice to see you again."

Britton looked up to see her sister standing beside their table with Daphne next to her. She swore she saw Daphne's eyes grow dark with anger as she stared at her.

"You too," Victoria said. "I hear you're getting married soon, congratulations."

"Thank you. Oh, pardon my manners. This is my maid of honor and best friend, Daphne," Bridget said.

"It's nice to meet you," Victoria said.

Daphne pulled her eyes away from Britton and smiled at Victoria.

"What are you guys doing here?" Britton said.

"We went for the sizing of my dress this afternoon and decided to come here afterwards. I'll let you get back to dinner. I saw you come in and I wanted to say hi. Don't forget you and Daphne have your dress fittings this weekend," Bridget said.

"We have them for Heather's wedding too," Daphne added.

"I'll be there," Britton replied, a little sarcastically.

"That's the Daphne that you can't stand?" Victoria asked when they walked away.

"Yes. She's a righteous bitch."

"She's cute."

"She's a bitch."

~

Britton was glad to finally be home. She walked into her apartment, kicked her shoes off at the door, and began stripping out of her pantsuit. Dinner with Victoria had turned out to be nicer than expected, but she had politely refused when Victoria asked her over afterwards. She honestly didn't want to go back down that road again.

Once she finished changing clothes, Britton sat at her dining room gluing pieces of the model together. She worked on half of it at home in the evenings and the other half during the day in her office. When her cell phone rang she figured it was Victoria trying to entice her to come over, but the caller ID flashed: Heather Cell.

"Hey," Britton said, pushing the speaker phone button.

"So, you were out with Victoria, huh."

"How do you know that?" Britton said, gluing the pieces of the parking lot to the base of the model.

"Daphne called to confirm the time for the dress fitting Saturday," Heather said.

"Sure she did. It's none of her fucking business who I'm out with. God, she's such a pain in my ass."

"I take it things aren't getting any better between you two."

"Nope. She hasn't changed."

"Uh-huh. So, I thought it was over with Victoria."

28

"It is. I didn't go home with her when she asked. We actually just had a nice dinner together. She wants to try to be friends. I can tell she wants more, but it's never going to happen. I've finally learned my lesson."

"Be careful. I don't trust her crazy ass."

Britton laughed. "I don't trust your cousin."

"Daphne's harmless."

"Okay, wait until this weekend and see it for yourself. She acts like she wants to claw my eyes out when she's around me. Even tonight when she and Bridget came up to our table, she was looking at me like a woman scorned."

Heather laughed.

"I'm serious."

"Alright, alright. I'll pay attention this weekend."

"Good. Now, let me get back to this model. I think I just glued my fucking fingers together," Britton said, hanging up the phone as Heather laughed again.

She ran into the bathroom, running hot water over her fingers to separate them. It wasn't the first time she'd glued her fingers and surely not the last. Thankfully, hot water worked as a solvent on the bonding gel they used for the models.

29

Chapter Five

The rest of the week went by in a blur. On top of working on the project for her father, Britton was assisting on two other proposals. At the end of the day on Friday, all she wanted to do was kick her feet up, but she'd promised Heather's fiancé Greg, that she would go to his bachelor party. In a haste, Britton rushed home, changed into jeans, a low-cut, sleeveless black top, and black leather ankle-boots. She sprayed a little perfume on her wrists and neck and checked the mirror one last time. Her wavy hair looked windblown and sexy. She was ready for a night on the town with a bunch of rowdy guys.

The party bus arrived in front of her apartment building as she was locking her door. She made sure her ID was in one of her back pockets with her phone in the other. She patted the wad of cash in her front pocket and stuffed her house key in the other front pocket. Greg's brother Dennis jumped out to greet her. He was Greg's best man and in charge of the evening's festivities.

Everyone knew he had a thing for Britton, but everyone knew she was a lesbian, including him.

"Are you ready to party until you can't stand up?" Dennis said.

Britton laughed. "I don't know if I want to go that far, but someone has to keep you boys in line. Besides, what self-respecting lesbian is going to turn down a night of tits and ass in her face at Providence's finest strip club?"

He shook his head and watched her ass move in her jeans as she walked ahead of him.

Britton took a seat near the back of the bus. The alcohol was flowing and she'd consumed two shots before the bus had even left her complex. She was in for a hell of a night.

Twenty minutes later, the bus pulled up in front of a VIP lounge called the Cat House. Everyone unloaded from the bus. Greg walked in the middle of the group with a big king's crown on his head. Britton stayed near the back as they entered the building and were shown to a private room with a stage that had three poles surrounded by big chairs and small side tables.

"My name is Daisy. I'll be your party host and server for the evening," a petite red-head said. She had pasties covering the nipples of her enhanced breasts and wore tiny cut-off shorts. She winked at Britton when she saw her bringing up the rear of the group.

As soon as everyone was situated, the curtain that doubled as a door to the room closed. Dennis passed around big, thick cigars to everyone and ordered a bottle of Johnny Walker Blue Label with ten shot glasses from Daisy. Three women walked through another curtain on the opposite side of the room, each taking a pole. The DJ changed the song and the women began climbing the poles, sliding up and down and spinning around as the men lit their cigars. Most of the men didn't smoke, but under special circumstances they all lit up. Britton wasn't a smoker either and the last time she'd smoked a cigar she had turned green. She set her cigar on the table, turning her attention to the women dancing.

The woman on the left and closest to her, had long blond hair down to her ass, fair skin, perky breasts with light pink nipples, and a black lace thong. The thick heels on her feet were clear and at least four inches high. The woman dancing on the middle pole was a Latina with wavy dark hair and mocha tanned skin. Her breasts were fake, but not as big as Daisy's ample bosom, and her nipples were dark. She wore a leather G-string and black heels similar to those of the other dancers. The last woman had light brown hair and semi-tanned skin with moderately sized breasts that hung naturally and light brown nipples. She wore a pink lace thong and thick black heels.

Daisy returned, pouring glasses of scotch for everyone.

"To Greg, may he have the night of his life and get his dick hard, as he says goodbye to the single life!" Dennis toasted and everyone cheered, throwing back the shot.

The women continued working the poles for a few more songs as the liquor flowed in the private room.

"I'm glad you came with us," Greg said, smiling.

"Me too," Britton replied, clinking her glass with his. She noticed for the first time that Greg's thinning blond hair and blue eyes reminded her a little bit of a young Woody Harrelson. His brother Dennis was close to ten years older than him at thirty-nine and although his hair wasn't thinning like Greg's it was starting to show gray highlights in the light brown coloring.

The dancers got off the stage and brought a chair up to the middle and made Greg sit in it. They danced all over him for several songs before dispersing into the group. Britton kept to herself to the side, watching the women dance. It wasn't her first time in a strip club. In fact, she and Greg had celebrated their birthdays together in the same strip club the year before since their birthdays were only three days apart.

The blond ran her hand over Britton's leg as she climbed into Greg's lap, gyrating to the music. Britton laughed knowing the way the women danced on men was too forceful to be arousing. She waved Daisy over, asking her to bring some ice to the room. Warm scotch wasn't very appealing to her, so she hoped it was better with ice in it.

"Why are you hiding over here in the corner?" the Latina woman asked, spreading Britton's thighs so she could stand between them.

"Just watching," Britton commented, allowing the woman to sit in her lap.

"See something you like?" the dancer teased.

"Maybe."

"Don't let her fool you," Greg yelled from across the small room. "She eats pussy better than we do!"

Britton laughed, shaking her head.

The dancer smiled with a raised eyebrow. "Do you want a dance?"

"Sure," Britton said, sliding back in the chair to give the woman room as she climbed up on her.

The dancer moved her body against Britton in slow, seductive movements that were completely opposite of the loud thrashing beat of the song playing. She rubbed her breasts over Britton's face and spun around so that she was sitting in Britton's lap, lying back against her with her head on her shoulder. She grabbed Britton's hands, running them up her thighs, over the leather G-string, across her taut stomach and up to her breasts. She squeezed her own breasts with Britton's hands and ran them back down her body. Then she turned back around, taking her shoes off, and stood in Britton's chair putting her crotch in Britton's face. She grabbed Britton's hands, put them on her ass, and ran her hands through Britton's hair as if she were giving her pleasure. A few of the guys noticed what was going on the corner and began cheering. She climbed down when the song was over and gave Britton a kiss on the cheek.

The next two hours of the night went by in a blur. Britton received dances from the other two women, as well as the Latina again before the night was over and she consumed more scotch than she'd ever thought possible.

The bus finally dropped her off at her apartment close to four a.m. and Britton stumbled inside. She couldn't remember the last time she had been that drunk and she knew she was going to feel like shit in the morning. She regretted telling Heather that ten o'clock was fine for the dress fitting the next morning.

Chapter Six

Britton barely had time to swing through Starbucks on her way to the dress shop. She ordered the largest coffee they had with three espresso shots and a huge muffin. She ground the gears of her sports car only once as she drove down the road, drinking and eating as fast as she could. She looked in the mirror at the bags under her eyes and put her dark sunglasses back on.

I'm still drunk, she thought and laughed.

By the time she arrived, Heather, her mom Claire, her step-mom Marianne, her step-sister Leslie, and Daphne were all at the dress shop waiting for her. She gulped down the last of the coffee, tossing the cup and wrapper from her muffin in the trash on the way inside.

Heather laughed at her best friend as soon as she saw her. Britton was wearing jeans, flip-flops, and a loose fitting brown top. Her hair had a very windblown but sexy look, because she'd ridden with the top down on the Porsche.

"Greg told me to tell you he's sorry," Heather said.

"Tell him to fuck off," Britton growled with a smile.

"How bad is it?" Heather asked out of earshot.

"I'm still drunk," Britton laughed. "God, this is so not me. I think those bastards did it on purpose."

"What the hell were you drinking?"

"Scotch."

"Gross!"

"You think?!"

"What's wrong with you?" Daphne asked when Heather and Britton made their way over to the group.

"She went out with Greg's bachelor party last night," Heather said.

"Oh honey, I could've told you not to do that," Claire, Heather's mom commented.

"Can we get this going so I can go back to bed?" Britton replied.

Daphne sneered. "Serves you right," she huffed under her breath loud enough for Britton to hear. "And what kind of hairstyle is that?"

"It's called just-fucked," Britton whispered to her.

Daphne gasped in shock.

"Oh good God, it's windblown. I rode with the top down on my damn car," Britton growled.

"Greg mentioned you guys went to the *Cat House*," Heather said.

"Yes."

Daphne looked appalled. Britton grinned at her.

"You can probably take your sunglasses off, Hon." Claire laughed, as the woman managing the dress shop walked over to them.

She was slightly round with short, graying hair. She wore dark slacks and a floral print top with a name tag on the right side that had the name Sandy printed on it.

"We have the dresses ready that you picked out. They're in the fitting room. Follow me," the woman announced, leading the group to the back of the store.

Heather went into Britton's fitting room with her, knowing she'd need a little help. Britton stripped down to her black satin bra and panties. The muscular body of the high school star athlete she'd been was still visible in her well-toned body.

"This is pretty. I love the color," Britton said, eyeballing the purple dress with spaghetti straps, a low neckline, and a crisscross design leaving the back open with a small slit up the back as well.

"Thanks. It took us hours to find the perfect dresses."

"I remember seeing the picture of this one," Britton said, stepping inside the dress. She pulled it up, slipping her arms through the straps.

Heather zipped the back of the dress and Britton turned towards her to look in the mirror.

"It looks great. How does it fit?"

"Fine," Britton said, turning to look at all of the sides in the mirror. "I like the fact that it isn't too long," she said, pointing out that the dress was only calf length.

"I wanted it to be something everyone could wear again."

"Where are the shoes?" Britton asked.

Heather opened a box that had white strappy shoes that look like sandals with a two inch heel on the back.

"Oh those look uncomfortable, but they're cute," Britton exclaimed.

"Actually, I bought a pair to try out and I love them. I'm taking them on the honeymoon."

Heather closed the straps when Britton slipped into the shoes.

"When everyone is dressed you can step out here in front of the large mirrors so we can take a look at everything," Sandy said.

"Don't bust your ass in those and rip the dress," Heather teased.

"Wouldn't that just be my luck?" Britton laughed. "I'm getting better. The gallon of coffee and giant muffin helped soak up some of the alcohol. My buzz is just about gone," she frowned.

"This reminds me of the time we snuck into Mr. Hoffmeyer's class still drunk from the night before." Heather laughed.

"Oh my God, I think that was the longest algebra class ever! I know I've never looked at quadratic equations the same," Britton teased.

They both laughed.

All of the women stepped out into the middle of the room and walked over to the platform surrounded by mirrors. They all looked at each other. Britton noticed Daphne giving her the once over and raised an eyebrow. Daphne gave her a snide look and turned away. Leslie was the only one who needed alterations. Her flat breasts were too small to fill in the top so it would need to be taken in.

"I think we should look at something else. This dress is okay, but I'm sure they have more that fit better," Marianne sneered.

Heather's mom went to say something, but Heather turned towards the woman she had dubbed step-monster. "This is the dress that was chosen. There is plenty of time for alterations for anyone that needs them."

"Go ahead and ring up these dresses and shoes," Claire told Sandy. "Include her alterations as well," she said, nodding towards Leslie.

Leslie took the dress off quickly and she and her mother left.

"Ring her up some tits while you're at it," Britton said to Sandy who was out of ear shot.

Heather laughed and Daphne looked as embarrassed as a school girl who had just shown the class her panties. Claire snickered a little before walking over to the register.

"You're a mess." Heather laughed as she walked into the fitting room with Britton.

"What happened to the refined woman that wears Armani and drinks Perrier?" Heather asked.

"Do you see a Prescott here besides me?" Britton answered. "Anyway, you can't stand either one of them."

"True," Heather said when they walked out of the fitting room.

"I don't get a good signal in here. I'll be right back," Britton said walking towards the door with her phone. She wanted to call Greg and burn his ass since he was at home sleeping in while she had to endure the torture of dress shopping.

"Why do you have to be so uncensored? It's really unappealing," Daphne growled.

Britton raised an eyebrow. "Are you seriously talking to me?"

Daphne rolled her eyes, tucking a loose strand of hair behind her ear.

"Don't even start with me. You're the one that has issues, not me. Maybe if you took that stick out of your ass and lightened up a little bit your life wouldn't be so fucking miserable. Tell Heather I'll call her later," Britton said, storming across the parking lot to her car. She'd had enough of Daphne's bitchy attitude.

~

The next afternoon, Britton showed up at the dress shop on the other side of town with a minute to spare. She slid out of her car and pushed the door shut. The wind whipped her hair around her shoulders as she walked across the parking lot.

Daphne stood out of sight and near a window, watching her walk towards the store. Britton looked completely different than she had the day before. The jeans and flip -lops were replaced by tan slacks and dark brown sandals and the oversized shirt was replaced by a sleeveless white button-down blouse.

"You're late," Bridget said.

Britton grinned. "It's good to see you too," she said looking at her sister. She was surprised by how much she looked like their mother more and more every day. They shared the same brown eyes, high cheek bones, multi-colored blond hair and slender, petite build.

"I heard how you showed up to Heather's dress fitting yesterday."

"I'm sure you've heard a lot of things!" Britton said, loud enough for Daphne to hear as she pretended to look through the dresses on racks.

"You should be ashamed of yourself," Bridget scolded.

"Yes, Hail Mary and all of that," Britton sighed.

"What's going on?"

"Hello mom. Bridget's just being a mother hen as usual," Britton said.

"The dresses are ready. Right this way, ladies," the sales woman said. She had a dark bob haircut and a slender figure. She wore a dark pantsuit and had a yellow measuring tape around her shoulders, reminding Britton of one of the girls she would see in Victoria's Secret in the mall waiting to measure her breasts for a new bra.

Britton stepped into the fitting room and eyed the canary yellow dress. The only thing she liked about it was the fact that it didn't have poufy sleeves. It was long, almost floor length, with wide straps for sleeves and a high neckline. The shoes were open-toed pumps with three-inch heels, dyed to match the dress. Britton sighed. This was definitely an ensemble she would never wear again. She loved her mother and sister, but they shared the same old-fashioned sense of style.

"What do you think?" Bridget said as Britton and Daphne stepped out of the fitting room and faced each other.

Britton bit the inside of her lip so hard it drew blood, to keep from laughing. Daphne refused to look Britton in the eyes.

"I love it," Daphne said.

Liar! Britton thought. She knew better. Daphne wasn't looking at her or making stupid comments because she wanted to laugh too.

"Great. It looks like we won't need any alterations," the sales woman said.

"That's because we have tits," Britton mumbled, under her breath.

"What was that?" her mother asked.

"I said, I love the way it fits."

Daphne raised an eyebrow, clearly having heard what Britton had actually said and the lie she told her mother.

"Let's get them wrapped up. Give me a call when the shoes are ready to be picked up. How long do you think it will take to dye them?" Sharon asked.

"Oh, it only takes about two days. You should be able to get them by Wednesday," the sales woman said.

Daphne and Britton went to the fitting rooms and changed back into their own clothes while Sharon and Bridget went to the register with the sales woman.

"I can't believe you," Daphne growled when Britton stepped out of her fitting room.

"What are you talking about?"

"I heard what you said. Are you ever going to grow up?"

Britton shook her head and sighed. "That stick up your ass has got to be uncomfortable," she said before walking away.

Daphne watched her leave. Britton's tailored clothes fit her body perfectly, revealing all of her natural curves as she walked.

Chapter Seven

By Wednesday of the following week, Britton was too tired to stand on her own two feet. Her father had called on Monday to say that he wanted her to bring the model into his office at the company headquarters the following week. It was pointless to argue with him, so she had to squeeze two weeks of work into less than a week. Her other work projects were neglected, but she needed this project to be perfect. Her father's approval on the design was a lot more than that. She wanted him to realize she was good at what she did and she wanted his respect as an architect and artist. This was her one and only chance to earn that.

Britton was pulling out of the parking garage downtown when her phone rang. She pushed the button on the console allowing the call to come through the car speaker system.

"This is Britton."

"You sound tired," Heather said.

"I am. What's up?"

"Are you just now leaving the office?"

"Yes."

"Britton, it's after nine."

"I can tell time," she sighed, shifting gears and maneuvering easily through the streets. Downtown Providence looked like a ghost town at that time of night.

"You're burning the candle at both ends, Hon," Heather said.

"I know, but my father made more changes to my design this week and I had to go back and fix them on the model."

"He needs to respect what you do and see it as the art that it is."

"I doubt that will ever happen. I think he's setting me up to fail so he can show me that I'm making a mistake."

"Britt, that's ridiculous."

"Yeah, but that's the way he operates. The funny thing is, he has no idea how good I am at what I do and I'm just as stubborn as he is. I plan to give him exactly what he wants including every single minor detail change that he's made and prove him wrong when I blow his mind."

"You're extremely smart and obviously very talented. He has to see that. I mean you're killing yourself to get this project done."

"I know, but damn it, I'm going to get this thing completed by Friday. I won't have time to work on it at all this weekend. Someone's having a bachelorette party that's going to take up all of my time." Britton smiled.

"Yeah, about that, do you think you and Daphne can get through a night without scratching each other's eyes out?"

"It depends on whether or not that bitch runs back to my sister with anymore of my business. She told her all about Greg's party and of course Bridget brings it up with me in front of mom. I swear, that woman hates my guts, Heather."

"What the hell did you do to her in high school? I mean Daphne and Bridget couldn't stand either of us because your mom made them take us with them everywhere and I know you took her place as the captain of the rowing team, but something else is causing her to be so hostile towards you."

I swore I'd never tell anyone, not even you, my best friend. "I don't know. Maybe she's crazy or something. Maybe she and Victoria should hang out."

"Uh-huh, what now?"

"She doesn't understand why I don't want to get back together. She thinks there is someone else. Honestly, I wish there was, but all of my time for the past month has been tied up with this project and these weddings. I probably wouldn't notice it if a naked super-model stepped out in front of my car at the moment."

"She needs to get the hint and move on with her life. Obviously, going to dinner with her wasn't the best idea."

"You think?!" Britton laughed.

"If you get that damn model finished by Friday then you'll have even more reason to celebrate Saturday night," Heather said.

"Exactly. Make sure you're at my place at four," Britton said. The bachelorette party was starting at her apartment, which was another reason she needed the project finished by Friday. She had no place to put it in her apartment and she needed to clean and decorate for the party so she wouldn't have time to work on it anyway.

"I know. You've told me at least ten times. Be there at four and dress to party. I wish you would tell me what we're doing or at least give me a hint."

"Heather, it's a bachelorette party. We're going to party!"

"I'm a little nervous. Do you remember when I went to Jan's bachelorette party a few years ago?"

"Is she the hygienist you work with?"

"Yes. Her sister planned the party and had a group of naked men come to her house and dance and she made this hunch-punch shit that was like 200 proof. Everyone was so drunk they couldn't drive home and their cousin, Donna, was so drunk she gave one of the dancers a blow job in the bathroom."

"Wow, yeah, I remember you telling me about it. You don't need to worry. There won't be any hunch-punch or naked men at my apartment. You can believe me when I tell you there has never been and never will be a naked man in my apartment as long as I live there."

Heather laughed. "Does that mean my party stripper is going to be a woman?"

"Hey, if you want to see tits and ass, you can gladly go with me to Wade's party next week. I'm sure it will be similar to Greg's."

"No thanks. I heard the stories and saw how bad off you were the next day."

Britton laughed. "I just pulled into my complex and the delivery dude is standing at my door with the dinner I ordered from the office."

"What did you order?"

"Sushi. They always take an hour and the one time I need the hour they are on time. That's the story of my life. Let me go so I can get my food before this kid drives off and I have to chase him down the damn road to get my dragon rolls. I'll call you Friday."

Heather laughed as Britton hung up.

Britton signed the credit card slip and rushed inside with her dinner. She set the bag on the empty dining room table and ate two rolls before running down the hall to change out of her pantsuit. She knew the last time she had eaten was at lunch, but she couldn't remember what time that was. It felt like maybe it was yesterday, she was so hungry. It was still weird seeing her table clear. She'd finally taken the model pieces she was working on at home into the office the day before to finish them along with the other pieces and then glue the entire thing together.

Almost done, she thought. In truth, she really was almost done. She needed to finish the last building of the three part model and do a few more touches to the parking lot, but the Friday deadline shouldn't be a problem.

Finished with her dinner, she poured a glass of wine and sat on the couch with her feet up. The only interesting thing she could find on TV was a documentary about sharks off the coast of Massachusetts. She watched the show until she fell asleep. She woke up two hours later with a kink in her neck from the couch, thinking sharks obviously weren't as interesting as she thought. It was almost one a.m. when she finally crawled into her bed.

Chapter Eight

Saturday arrived more quickly than anticipated. Britton was glad to have finished her project Friday, after staying at work an hour late. It was wrapped up and ready to be presented to the client, in this case her father, on Monday morning. She had just finished cleaning her apartment, setting up the pre-ordered food, and decorating. The guests were set to start arriving any minute with the bride-to-be arriving shortly after.

Britton went to the bathroom to look in the mirror one last time. She checked her cream colored halter top, making sure she didn't have too much cleavage showing. The light color contrasted nicely with her olive skin. She smoothed her hand over her black slacks and zipped up the black dress boots that gave her a couple inches of height and completed her outfit. Her hair was down around her shoulders in loose waves.

The doorbell rang seconds later and Britton wondered if maybe Daphne was going to be the first to arrive so she could give her approval since she hadn't been included in any of the planning. Britton looked at the distorted image through the peephole in the door and saw two women, both brunettes. She pulled the door open.

"Welcome, I'm Heather's maid of honor and best friend, Britton."

"I'm Jan, I think you and I have met before. This is Carrie. We work with Heather at the dentist's office," one of the brunettes said.

"Oh, that's right. We met a few years ago. Please, come in and make yourselves at home," Britton was about to close the door when Daphne appeared.

"You're already shutting the door in my face. This is going to be a wonderful afternoon and evening," Daphne growled.

"Oh good grief, leave your fucking claws outside. I'll kick your ass if you ruin this for Heather," Britton whispered harshly to her as Daphne walked in. "Welcome, please, make yourself at home," she said a little louder and with a fake smile.

She chided herself for actually looking at Daphne as she crossed the room in gray cargo pants, a tight black blouse that was low-cut and rose up just enough to let the skin of her taut stomach peek out when she moved, and black strappy heels. Britton looked away when Daphne caught her staring.

Heather's step-sister, Leslie, was next to arrive, then her mother, followed by a few other friends, rounding out the group to a total of twelve people.

"Heather should be here any minute. Please help yourselves to the food and champagne," Britton said loudly, checking her watch.

The bride-to-be arrived right on time and was surprised to see everyone inside of Britton's apartment. Britton handed her a glass of champagne.

"Here's to a magical night for my best friend. I love you more than my own sister," Britton toasted, clinking her glass to Heather's.

"Wow," Heather said, noticing the decorations as she made her way around the small room. "I've never seen so many penises in one room," she laughed, looking at the penises taped to the walls and statue penises on the tables.

Britton laughed. "I've never handled so many penile shaped things in my life. I must love you a lot to hang penises all over my apartment."

"I don't get it," Jan said.

"Britton's a lesbian," Heather said.

"No shit?!" Jan raised an eyebrow. "I would've never guessed."

"Me either," one of the other women said.

"I promise, I'm a card carrying dyke," Britton joked.

"Her flannel shirts and tool belt are in the closet and she's wearing a huge eight-inch strap-on dildo under those designer slacks. Do you want to see it?" Heather teased, looking directly at Leslie.

"What?!" Leslie's jaw hit the floor. She was so nervous she almost spilled the glass of champagne she was holding.

"Leslie, it's huge," Heather said holding her hands a foot apart mimicking the size she was referring to.

"Oh my God, Heather, you're scaring everyone. She's kidding." Britton laughed. "I am a lesbian though, yes. Anyway, my sexual preferences aren't the reason we're all here. Now, drink these expensive bottles of champagne that I bought and eat that wonderful delivery food that I ordered because the limo will be here in a little while to pick us up."

"What? Where are we going? I thought the party was here," Daphne said from the corner of the room.

"It's a surprise and something that just might loosen that stick," Britton said with a wink.

A few of the women began whispering about where they thought the group was going. Daphne's eyes shot daggers at Britton before she turned her back to her.

"Don't egg her on," Heather said.

"Oh really, like you egging on Leslie?"

"What are you talking about?"

"You were trying to get a rise out of her. I'm wearing a strap-on? Really? And you know better than to think you would find anything flannel in my closet."

Heather laughed and Britton shook her head with a smile.

"So, where are we going?"

Britton shrugged.

"Come on, tell me. And why aren't you drinking as much as I am? You need to get to my level."

Britton laughed. "Someone has to stay somewhat sober to keep this group in line."

"Uh-huh. Don't worry about what Daphne reports back to your sister. Do you want me to say something to her?"

"No. I want you to go eat. I take it you haven't eaten all day if you have a buzz from two glasses of champagne. You're going to be in for a long night at this rate."

"Yes, mom," Heather teased.

A few more guests arrived late and the bridal shower finally kicked off. Britton figured it was easier just to have a quick bridal shower and then head off to the bachelorette party that same evening. Everyone watched as Heather opened box after box of lingerie, as well as a custom-made photo album, and a pile of kitchen and home items from her wedding registry. Britton had already given them her gift a week early: a package of spa visits to a very high-end spa in town with multiple days that she could use at her leisure. Heather still didn't know how to thank her best friend. It was a gesture she would never forget since going to a spa was something she had always wanted to do and it was at the top of her bucket list.

By six o'clock, the shower guests had left and the seven people who remained were ready to start the bachelorette party. Twenty minutes later, a white limo arrived. Britton walked outside and spoke to the driver briefly before going back inside.

"Listen up, ladies, I figured instead of sitting here all night playing pin the dick on the stud, or telling dirty stories, you would rather go to a male revue show and let the men dance on you until your panties melt off," Britton said.

A few women hooted and others cheered.

Britton opened the door. "The car is outside," she said, fanning her arms out.

"Wow, this is going to be fun!" Heather said to her.

"I figured Greg had tits swinging in his face the other night, so why not have a few penises swinging in yours tonight," Britton said to her.

"Sweet!" Heather squealed and ran out to the car.

They arrived at the club quickly and went inside to the table at the front near the stage. Everyone ordered a drink and waited patiently. As soon as their drinks arrived, the lights went down and thumping music throbbed through the sound system. Smoke billowed from the stage as six men walked out wearing suits like those in the Men in Black movies. They danced in sync to the beat of the music, removing pieces of clothing here and there, until they were wearing nothing but a G-string that barely covered their parts.

Britton watched the women at the table cheering and waving dollar bills. Heather had an ear to ear smile on her face and multiple dollars in her hands. She noticed Daphne was watching the show, but hadn't cracked a smile and wasn't on the edge of her seat like everyone else.

Good grief. Is she that much of a prude that she can't have a little fun at a male dancer show? Britton thought.

The men went backstage at the end of the song and came back out in another costume, dancing in sync once again. At the end of the second song they called Heather and one other bachelorette up to the stage where they set them in chairs. They took turns dancing on the two women, rubbing themselves all over them, and making sure they ran the women's hands over their bodies. At the end of the song, they sent the women back to their seats and dispersed into the crowd to dance around the tables allowing women to put money in their thongs.

One guy in particular came over to their table and pulled Britton's chair back. He straddled her legs, rubbing his hardness over her thigh and against her crotch. She smiled and went along with it. When he moved his face closer to hers she whispered in his ear.

"I'll give you a hundred dollars to pull the blond at the end of the table on the stage with another guy and show her a good time."

"No problem," he said, kissing her on the cheek as she tucked the large bill into his thong near his penis.

"I thought you were a lesbian?" Leslie said.

"It's all in good fun. It doesn't mean I want to go home and fuck him because he danced on me," Britton said, laughing. Heather rolled her eyes and opened her legs for another dancer who walked up to her.

The men finally went back to the stage for another performance and two of them came out dressed as cops and looking for the bad girls in the audience. One of the guys grabbed Daphne by the hand and led her up the steps. Heather elbowed Britton and nodded towards the stage. Britton laughed.

"What did you do?" Heather asked.

"Nothing. Maybe this will finally loosen that stick in her ass," Britton said, watching as the two men danced all over Daphne.

They rubbed themselves all over her arms, thighs, and crotch as they undressed. They ran her hands all over their bodies, making sure she handled their weapons too. Daphne had a polite smile on her face and seemed very nervous, almost embarrassed.

"She looks scared to death," Heather said.

Britton was laughing so hard she started choking on her drink.

When the dance was over, Daphne exited the stage and walked around the table towards her seat at the opposite end.

"How's that stick now?" Britton asked loudly as she passed by.

Daphne spun around to face her with a look that made Britton recoil as if she'd just been slapped.

"Oh, she's pissed," Heather snickered.

"Serves her right," Britton grinned.

The show ended a half hour later and the women piled back into the limo.

"Where are we going now?" Heather asked.

Britton shrugged. "Wherever the driver takes us, I guess."

The driver already had instructions to take them to one of the upscale night clubs. He maneuvered the long white car through the streets, coming to a stop in front of the club a few minutes later. The women got out and looked up at the building.

"Dancing anyone?" Britton said to the group as she led them towards the VIP entrance.

The group of woman pushed two high top tables together near the end of one of the bars as Britton ordered a round of shots for everyone.

"This is the best night of my life," Heather said.

Britton smiled brightly. "I'm glad you're having fun."

"I'm pacing myself. I don't want to get completely loaded. I want to remember this."

The women went out on the floor and danced to a few thumping techno songs and returned to the table for their drinks. No one noticed Victoria stagger up to them.

"I'm over you," Victoria sneered in Britton's face, loud enough for the group to hear. Then, she looked at Daphne. "I know your little secret and if you want Britton so bad you can fucking have her!"

Daphne stormed off towards the bathroom.

"Go to hell, Victoria," Britton yelled.

Everyone at the table sat with their mouths wide open as Victoria stumbled away laughing.

"What the fuck just happened?" Heather asked.

"Victoria, being Victoria. Now, you know why I'm single and choosing to stay that way," Britton sighed. "She's crazy. I have no idea what the hell she was talking about."

"Who was that?" Jan asked.

"Britton's crazy ass ex-girlfriend," Heather said.

Britton got up from the table and went in search of Daphne. She finally found her in the back bathroom sitting in a stall, crying.

"Daphne?" Britton called out.

Daphne stood up and walked out of the stall, wiping the tears from her eyes.

"Why did you tell her?!" she growled.

"I didn't say anything to her."

"Then why the hell did she say what she said? I can't believe you. You're such a fucking bitch and a spoiled daddy's girl to boot. You're pathetic!" she yelled.

"Daphne, I swear to you. I never said anything to her about you. As far as she knows we hate each other's guts and she has no idea why. She said all of that stuff to hurt us both. She's jealous and thinks I'm in love with you or that you want me or some twisted shit like that. She's crazy. That's why we're not together and haven't been for a few months."

"You were just out with her!"

"I'm not dating her. We had dinner together, that's all. The woman is nuts. I'm sorry this happened."

"Are you? It sure looks like you're having a great time at my expense tonight."

"You want to hate me, then fine. I can't stop you. You've hated me for years, but I never said anything to anyone and never will. It's not my story to tell, Daphne," Britton said harshly and walked out of the room.

"I'm sorry that crazy bitch ruined your night," Britton said to Heather as she sat back on her stool.

"I'm fine. She's gone and it's over. Why did she say that shit about Daphne?"

"She swears I'm seeing someone else or at least wants to. She thinks it's Daphne."

"That's stupid. Daphne's not a lesbian first of all and you two hate each other. That's the last hook-up to ever happen on earth. If you two had to get together to save mankind the world would die," Heather laughed.

Britton clinked glasses with her in agreement.

~

An hour later, the limo dropped the women off at Britton's apartment. Everyone hugged Heather and thanked Britton for a wonderful night, all except Daphne. She hugged Heather and got in her car, driving off before some of the women could find their car keys.

Heather went inside the apartment and flopped down on the couch. She was glad she was staying the night. Her head was spinning and there was no way she could drive.

"Go get in the spare bed, Hon. You don't want to sleep on that couch, trust me," Britton said, helping her friend off the couch.

"Why aren't you drunk?" Heather asked.

"I have a buzz. I'm good. This was your night."

"If I ever see Victoria again I'm going to hit her over the head with my shoe," Heather slurred. She was trying to get her clothes off.

Britton laughed. "Okay, you do that," she said, helping her undress. "Get some sleep. I'll see you in the morning with a big cup of coffee, a couple of Advil, and a greasy breakfast."

Britton walked to her room at the other end of the hall and changed into a plum-colored silk pajama top with spaghetti straps and matching tiny pajama shorts that barely covered her ass, with nothing under them. She pulled the covers back on her bed and crawled inside. Her mind kept drifting back to Daphne and her secret. She hadn't thought of that day in almost ten years.

It had been a hot summer that year in Rhode Island and on a sunny Saturday afternoon Britton and Heather were out in the bay rowing. They were sophomores and Britton was the captain of their high school rowing team. Rowing was Britton's life. She lived for the feel of slicing through the water in a rowing scull.

After four hours of rowing all over the bay, Britton headed home. She knew her parents were going to some gala benefit and wouldn't be home until late that night. She thought of staying over at Heather's, but decided to go home. She was in desperate need of a shower, especially after walking home from the nearby marina where they kept their practice scull.

Britton walked into the quiet house, running straight up to her room. She kicked her shoes off and removed her tank top as she moved across the room. She entered her bathroom, pulling her sports bra over her head, revealing the well-defined muscles of her athletic body and summer sun-tanned skin as a loud shriek echoed in the room. Britton froze.

Standing only a few feet away, naked and wet from her shower, was Daphne Atwood. Britton watched Daphne's eyes roam over her body and stop on her chest. She raised an eyebrow, taking a step closer to her. She cleared her throat and Daphne's eyes shot up to hers.

"Why the hell are you standing naked in my bathroom?" Britton asked.

"I...you...I..." Daphne stumbled over her words, slightly moving forward.

Britton met her eyes once again, gazing questioningly as she closed the gap between them. Daphne's wet lips met her own softly as their breasts pressed together. The water dripping from Daphne's wet body pooled between them where their skin connected. Britton opened her mouth, tasting Daphne's lips and tongue as Daphne wrapped her arms around Britton, pulling her tightly against her. This was like nothing Britton had ever felt before. Daphne wasn't the first girl she'd kissed and her family knew she was gay, but the way Daphne felt naked against her made her so wet she could barely stand up.

Daphne pulled away abruptly, gasping for air. The cool air of the bathroom burned Britton's sensitive lips. It took a second for her ears to register that Bridget was calling for Daphne from down the hall. Britton watched in silence as Daphne hastily wrapped the towel around herself and ran out of the room without looking back.

Chapter Nine

Britton found herself standing in the small conference room of the current Prescott's Grocery Store headquarters. The room was small, with a large oval table and ten chairs around it taking up most of the space. She picked a piece of lint from the sleeve of her black pantsuit jacket and looked at the four model pieces on the table with a smile on her face. She had poured her heart and soul into that project and was proud to show it off. Her father's booming voice in the hallway turned her attention to the door.

Stephen Prescott entered the room, still talking on his cell phone. He smiled at his youngest daughter and Britton returned the gesture. Her father was dressed in a dark suit with a white shirt and a red tie with the blue company logo in the center.

"I'm sorry. I had to take that call," Stephen said, walking over to give his daughter a hug.

"So, here is your new building," Britton said, fanning her hand over the table. "This is the entire building here."

She pointed to the large modern-looking, rectangle shape that was a scaled replica of the full building and parking lot.

Her father nodded.

"These three pieces here are a cut-away of each floor. You will notice colonial style pillars and columns throughout each floor. The first floor, here, has the reception desk and waiting area in the front. The outside rooms, all around the reception area, are for your sales managers, district managers, and so on and the mailroom is in the back, next to a small break room and bathroom. The second floor, over here, has the large conference room and the accounting offices, along with two bathrooms and a small break room. The top floor, right here, has all of the upper management offices and secretary areas, including your oval office, and two bathrooms with a small break room. The parking lot is designed to be one way in and one way out circling around and there is a gazebo behind the back of the building for smokers or anyone who may want to enjoy their lunch outside, overlooking the bay." She finished presenting each piece and stepped back to let her father take it all in.

"This looks different from the sketch," he said, studying the first floor cut-away.

"It's almost identical to the sketch I faxed you after we discussed that cubicles are fine for a call center, but not a company headquarters. I changed the faxed sketch a little bit and made the entrance area larger. I still put offices along the sides like you saw in the design."

He examined each piece thoroughly. The building was everything he wanted and more.

"I don't know what to say, Britton."

"Is something wrong? I can make more changes." *This is turning into a huge waste of time*, she thought.

"No...no changes." He stared at the completed building, looking at it from every angle. "It reminds me of something your grandfather would have wanted. He always said this building we are in now needed to feel more welcoming and comfortable. After all, we are a family business. I think he would be proud of you. Hell, I'm proud of you." He paused for a moment. "I tell you what, get Kevin and Suanne to help you carry all of these down to the main conference room. I want to unveil it at the quarterly meeting this afternoon."

Britton was speechless. "Okay, yeah...sure."

Her father smiled and gave her a hug.

"I'm glad you like it, daddy."

He smiled before walking out of the room.

Britton sat down in one of the chairs, breathing a sigh of relief. She'd thought for sure she had failed her father once again. Maybe he was finally starting to open his eyes a little bit to the idea of her having her own career. At least this was her way of contributing to the family business.

~

Britton went to her sister's office after she finished moving the model pieces and setting them up for the unveiling.

"Hey, you have a minute?" Britton asked, popping her head inside the small office. Bridget's desk was covered with stacks of papers.

"Hey, yeah...come in. So," Bridget sat back in her chair with her eyebrows raised. "Did he like it?"

"I think I shocked him."

"Why?"

"He said my design is something grandpa would've wanted. He also told me he's proud of me."

"That's great, Britt! Where is it? I want to see it!"

"It's in the conference room downstairs. Daddy's going to unveil it at the end of the meeting today."

"Damn. I might sneak down there and take a peek at it."

"Don't get caught," Britton laughed. "I'll see you later."

~

Britton spent the rest of the morning and early afternoon at her drawing desk. Finally having her father's approval gave her the confidence to take on another solo proposal for the firm. This one was a law office that was more intricately detailed, but smaller in size than the building she had designed for her father. She drew the scaled base and was working on the full exterior when she realized what time it was.

Britton rushed through town, squeezing her car into what seemed like the last parking space anywhere near the Prescott's office building. She walked into the packed conference room and moved to a spot in the corner.

"Speaking of my daughter," Stephen said, motioning to the back of the room. "As I said, Prescott's is about to break ground on a brand new headquarters building that really defines this company's past, present, and future. I'm honored to say that it was designed by my daughter, Britton Prescott." He waved her to the front of the room.

Together they pulled the black cloth off the designs. "I present to you, the new foundation of Prescott's Grocery."

Everyone in the room clapped their hands with excitement.

"She knows more about this than I do, so I'll let her tell you about it." He smiled, stepping out of the way.

Britton cleared her throat. She hadn't expected him to allow her to make the presentation to the company. She wasn't even an employee.

"Well, good afternoon everyone," she said, smiling as she looked at the group of men and women. Her eyes briefly stopped on Daphne. She was wearing a white button-down blouse with three-quarter sleeves and black slacks. The small diamond earrings she wore sparkled in the fluorescent lighting of the room.

Britton turned her attention back to the model. "This larger piece here is the full-scale model of the facility and these other three pieces are the three different floors. The top floor is for upper management, the middle floor is for accounting, and the bottom floor is for reception and store operations."

"Let's give her a round of applause. This concludes today's meeting, ladies and gentlemen. Please, come up and take a look at the new headquarters on your way out. I will see everyone bright and early tomorrow morning."

Britton stood near the table explaining different sections and answering questions as everyone gathered around to see the new building.

"This is amazing, Britt!" Bridget exclaimed.

"Thanks." Britton smiled.

"I'm impressed. I had no idea you were this talented," Daphne said.

"Yeah, well, there's a lot you don't know about me," Britton replied sarcastically. "Excuse me," she said, walking away.

Britton saw her father heading for the room's exit.

"Thanks, daddy." She wrapped her arms around him.

"I should be saying that to you. Everyone's excited. I guess I need to cut you a check." He smiled.

"It would be nice to get paid, yes, but I'm really glad you like it."

"I still think you're making a huge mistake."

"I know," she said.

"I'll have the first check drafted and sent to your office tomorrow. How soon do you think we can have all of the permits?"

"I'll check with the office, but probably by the first of April."

"Great." He hugged her again and walked towards the stairs to go up to his office.

Britton turned to the opposite way and started walking towards the exit. She wasn't an employee and really had no reason to hang around. She spun around on her heels when she heard someone call her name.

"Can we talk?" Daphne said, walking towards her.

"About what?" Britton said.

"I...uh...I just wanted to tell you, I don't hate you."

"That's nice, but you could've fooled me." Britton raised an eyebrow, wondering where this conversation was going and where it had come from.

"You're an amazing artist."

"What's wrong with you? Are you feeling okay? You're being nice to me."

"I'm fine, Britton. I guess, I don't know." She tucked a loose strand of hair behind her ear. "This weekend really opened my eyes when you said I hated you. I guess all of the hostility I've had towards you would make you think that, but I don't hate you."

"Then why the hell are you such a bitch?!"

"Britton, you harbor a secret that could have easily ruined my life all of these years."

"That's no reason to treat me like shit."

"Well, you haven't exactly been nice to me either," Daphne said.

"That's because you've been a royal bitch to me since I was fifteen years old!"

"I'm sorry. I just..well I wanted you to know it wasn't fueled by anger."

Britton nodded and began to walk away. She turned around just before she reached the door. Daphne was still standing in the same spot, looking at her.

"Do you want to have dinner with me?" Britton asked.

"Uh..." Daphne just stared at her.

"Is that a yes or a no?"

"I...guess. Yes. Let me grab my notebook and purse. I'll meet you out front."

Britton walked out to her car and slid into the seat. *What the hell are you thinking? This woman is your nemesis. She's a bitch and she hates you. Okay, she doesn't hate you, but she severely dislikes you,* she thought.

"What the hell did I invite her to dinner for?"

"Huh?" Daphne said.

Britton didn't realize she was already at the car with the passenger door opened.

"Nothing...so where do you want to eat?" Britton asked.

"I don't care. What do you like to eat?"

Britton shrugged. "I eat just about anything. Have you ever been to Schooner's? It's a seafood place across town."

"No. That's fine with me."

Britton nodded and drove out of the parking lot.

"This is a nice car," Daphne said, noting the sleek, black leather interior as she watched Britton shift gears out of the corner of her eye.

"Thanks. It was my gift to myself when I graduated MIT," Britton said, changing lanes.

"I forgot you went there. I guess I really don't know anything about you, at least not anymore."

"Nope." Britton glanced at her. "I'm all grown up, now."

"I see that."

"If it's any consolation, I know nothing about you either. When Bridget mentions you I tend to ignore her," Britton exclaimed.

Daphne laughed. "I guess I gave you a lot of reasons for that."

"You think?"

"It wasn't just me you know. You weren't exactly nice to me all of these years either."

Britton pulled up to the valet. "Could you blame me? Let's just agree that we have a mutual dislike for each other."

"If that's true, then why are we about to go inside this restaurant and have dinner together?"

Britton was about to answer when the valet attendant opened her door. She eyed the young man suspiciously, but reluctantly handed him her keys and walked around the back of the car. Daphne was already standing on the sidewalk.

"Are you going to answer me?" Daphne asked.

"I don't know why. Do you want to go have dinner or not? Before that kid takes my car for a joy ride," Britton said, watching her car. "Maybe this was a mistake."

"Maybe it was, but we might as well go inside and eat."

Britton silently followed her inside where they were shown to a booth in the back. Both women quickly ordered a glass of wine and opened their menus.

This woman drives me crazy, Britton thought, peering over her menu at the blond sitting across from her.

"What's wrong?" Daphne asked, eyeing Britton suspiciously.

Britton sighed. "I guess I'm waiting for the claws to come out. I don't understand why you had a sudden change of heart."

"I didn't come to dinner to fight with you, Britton. Something made me believe you when you said you never told that woman my secret. I think it was when you said I hated you all of these years." She raised her hand when Britton tried to rebut. "Let me finish. I don't expect us to become best friends overnight or over one dinner, but I want you to know I never hated you. Now, what's good here? That rubber chicken lunch your father served us was horrible."

"Huh," Britton flustered.

"I'm assuming you've been here before," Daphne looked up at her with raised eyebrows.

"I had the catch of the day. I'm sure everything is good," Britton said, happy to see the waitress return with their drink order. She quickly drank a long swallow of the buttery-oak flavored wine.

They ordered their meal and as they ate Britton listened to Daphne talk about working at Prescott's and living in New Bedford. They kept the conversation very basic for the rest of the evening.

Britton watched Daphne when she talked. She had always wondered why someone as beautiful as Daphne could be such a bitch. *Maybe this is a new beginning,* she thought. *It still doesn't mean I'm going to admit I'm attracted to her.*

Chapter Ten

The next afternoon, Britton sat at the drawing desk in her office trying to get her mind to focus on the project she was working on. She kept thinking about her dinner with Daphne. The evening had turned out better than she ever expected and she actually enjoyed herself. She was still shocked at the turn of events. Britton pushed her chair back with a heavy sigh. *Maybe some lunch will get my head out of this fog,* she thought.

She was just about to leave when her cell phone rang. She answered it on her way out of the office.

"Have you had lunch yet?" Heather asked.

"I'm leaving now."

"Me too. Where are you going?"

"I don't know. I'm not really hungry," Britton said, getting into her car.

"What's wrong?"

"Nothing. I love you to death, but I will be glad when all of this wedding crap is over and behind me."

"Uh-oh. What happened now?"

That was just it, Britton didn't really know what had happened. All of a sudden, it felt like everything had shifted, like the earth had changed the angle of its axis.

"Nothing really." Britton sighed. "I need to go run some errands on my lunch break. I'll call you later. Maybe we can get together for dinner or something," she said before hanging up.

Britton stopped at a book store looking for the latest design magazines and books on historical buildings. She often used them for inspiration. She was leaving the last store, lunch completely forgotten, when her phone rang again.

Figuring it was Heather calling back, she answered right away.

"I'm sorry."

"What are you sorry for?" Daphne said.

Britton's back stiffened when she heard the playful voice on the other end. "Uh...hey. I thought you were Heather."

"Oh. Anyway, I was calling to see what you were doing tonight."

"Not much, probably getting take-out and looking through the new books and magazines I just bought. Why?"

Britton was still surprised by Daphne's call.

"I wanted to repay you for buying dinner last night, but if you have plans..."

"Have you ever had Ying's?"

"Yes, I eat wings. Who doesn't?"

"No, not wings. Ying's!" Britton said loudly.

Daphne laughed. "Uh...no. What's Ying's?" she said, putting emphasis on the word Ying.

"It's a very good Chinese restaurant that is sort of like P.F. Chang's, but it's take-out or delivery only."

"Oh. Never heard of it."

"I was planning on getting delivery. Do you want come over?"

"I...yeah sure. Our meetings will be finished around five."

"Okay, see you then," Britton said, hanging up. *What has gotten into me?*

~

Britton's apartment was always clean. She didn't have any pets, she always washed her dishes immediately, and she never left clothes lying around. Still, she left the office a few minutes early to make sure her apartment was company ready. In reality, she was nervous. She figured the casual dinner she'd shared with Daphne the night before was a fluke and the next time she saw her she'd be back in bitch mode. The impromptu call from Daphne had thrown her for a loop and she was still surprised that she'd irrationally invited her over for take-out.

Britton finished changing from her pantsuit into jeans and a soft cotton shirt. She padded across the apartment barefooted when the doorbell rang, loving the way the plush carpet squished between her toes.

Daphne was standing in the doorway wearing stone-colored Capri pants, a white short-sleeved, low-cut blouse, and backless sandals with a small heel.

"I brought a change of clothes with me today," Daphne said, noticing Britton give her the once over.

"Come in," Britton said, stepping aside.

Daphne stepped inside. The apartment hadn't changed since she was there a few short days ago, except for the model pieces and drawings covering the kitchen table. She walked over to them.

"These weren't here Saturday."

"No, I brought them home last night. I usually work at home in the evenings and on the weekends," Britton said as she started gathering the pages to move them to the side.

Daphne grabbed her wrist. "Don't put them away on my account. I would love to see them."

"Okay...they're just rough sketches, really, nothing exciting," Britton said. She moved away from the table, rubbing her arm where Daphne had touched her. Her skin was much warmer in that spot.

"I'm intrigued by your artwork. You're very talented, Britton," Daphne said, thumbing through the drawings.

"Thanks." She thought for a moment, "If you like those then you will probably love these," she said, motioning for Daphne to follow her down the hallway.

Britton opened the door to her bedroom and nodded for Daphne to walk inside.

"Wow, your furniture is beautiful," Daphne conveyed, running her hand over the footboard of the cherry-colored sleigh bed.

Britton pointed to the wall on the opposite side of the room where four large drawings hung in matted frames.

"Oh my," Daphne walked over to the wall to get a closer look.

"This is the Natural History Museum in London," Britton said, pointing to the first picture of a building with two tall towers and multiple arched windows and triangle roof tops. The center of the picture was the huge archway leading to the main doors.

Daphne stepped over to the next picture. This building was smaller with a series of rectangle and arched windows across the front. Five statues adorned the points of the roof.

"This is The Paris Opera," Britton said.

The next picture was an old church with ornate windows and multiple pointed towers.

"That's a Transfiguration Church in Russia that was built during the Romanov Dynasty. It's a museum now."

"It's beautiful," Daphne said. "They're all...amazing."

"Thanks. This last one was the most difficult to capture," Britton added, pointed at the large castle-like structure with multiple towers and windows. It looked like it was built right on top of a mountain as if it was part of the mountain.

"It's majestic. Where is it?"

"Universal Studios Island of Adventure in Florida."

Daphne turned with a puzzled look on her face.

"It's the Hogwart's Castle from the Harry Potter movies and books," Britton declared, sheepishly. She shrugged. "I think it's an architectural masterpiece."

"I have to admit I've never read the books or seen the movies, but this does look magnificent. All of these pictures are astounding, Britton. I'm assuming you drew them."

"Yes. The summer before my senior year I traveled for three months sketching buildings and taking thousands of photos. I used these four pictures for my senior project."

"I hope you got an 'A'."

"Yes," Britton smiled. "I graduated with honors and was on the Dean's List all four years. My graduation project for my master's is actually on display at the school. We had to design and build a small city. It basically took the entire year to sketch and build. I made a city the makers of Star Wars would be proud of. It's titled Mysteria and it's a series of floating buildings of all shapes and sizes that are all attached in one way or another with wavy bridges or gangplanks. The buildings have a lot of windows and doorways and no two are the same. It's actually architectural chaos. It's designed to be a city that is in the year 3000 where cars fly and everything is suspended in space instead of grounded on earth. My professors were all blown away when I showed them the initial sketches. I thought they were going to tell me it was ridiculous and really in an architectural sense it is, but they were intrigued and gave me the go-ahead. So, I designed it and built it and the president of the school offered me money for it, but I turned away his money and donated it to the school."

"Are you serious? Bridget never mentioned that. Britton, that's wonderful. I would love to see it sometime."

"My family was there when it was unveiled as a donated piece of art to the school. My dad didn't care for it at all, but mom liked it. I have pictures of it."

"I'd love to see them," Daphne said.

"We should probably order dinner."

"Oh, yeah, I forgot about that," Daphne laughed.

"Besides, I'm sure you don't want to look at artwork all evening," Britton said, going to the Ying's menu that she kept in the kitchen. "Everything's good, so just pick whatever you want."

Daphne set the menu aside. "Britton, I'm intrigued by your artwork. You're a brilliant woman with a god-given talent. I wish I had known this side of you. I honestly never knew you were into art. All you and your family every talked about was rowing. When did everything switch to art?"

Britton smiled. "I took some art classes in school and realized I really enjoyed it. I was good at rowing and loved rowing, but drawing was my passion. My dad flipped out when I turned down all of the rowing scholarships to go to MIT for Architectural Design."

"I remember people talking about you going to the Olympics and one day heading Prescott's in his place."

"All his dreams, not mine."

"Wow."

"Not what you expected?" Britton asked.

"No. Well, I don't know. I spent so much time disliking you that I never got to really know you. Bridget used to talk about you here and there, but not often."

"You chose to dislike me all of these years instead of talking to me about what happened, Daphne. We were kids."

Daphne sighed, raising her eyes to Britton's slowly. "I didn't know how. I couldn't put it into words. It took me moving away from Rhode Island to finally be honest with myself."

"What do you mean?"

"I've been so hostile towards you all of these years because at first I blamed you."

"Wait a second, you were..."

"That's not what I mean. Trust me, I remember what happened and how it happened. I meant I blamed you for making me feel attracted to you. You were the first girl I was ever interested in sexually and I thought it was all your fault, that you made me this way. I went for years fighting an attraction I had no control over and I was so scared of being outed that I blamed you for everything that was fucked up in my life all of these years."

"Huh...wait...what?"

"I'm a lesbian, Britton. I have been for a while. I'm not out to my family or at work, but I live a pretty open life in New Bedford."

"Get the fuck out!" Britton was shocked. "Are you serious?!"

"Yes." Daphne smiled. "Britton, I've been treating you like shit all of these because I had feelings for you. I've had them since high school."

"Wow!" Britton was floored. She sat down on the couch. Her mind was still trying to process everything she just heard.

Chapter Eleven

"Say something. Anything," Daphne pleaded, sitting down next to Britton.

"I...I'm speechless." Britton looked at her, shaking her head. "Do you want some wine?" she asked, standing up.

"What?"

"Wine? I'm opening a bottle. Do you want a glass?" Britton questioned, walking towards the kitchen.

"Yeah, sure. I'd love one."

Britton opened a bottle of merlot and poured two glasses. She returned to the couch, handing Daphne one of them.

"So, all of this time, almost ten damn years, I thought you hated me and you actually had the hots for me," Britton said, still shaking her head.

"Something like that." Daphne laughed nervously.

"Why didn't you say anything to me?" Britton asked.

"I was confused and scared. Then, I graduated and went to college and barely ever saw you. Then, you graduated and moved away."

Britton put her head in her hands and laughed.

"I don't think it's that funny," Daphne chided.

"No. I'm not laughing at you, just the situation."

"When I saw you again at your parent's house in Newport I was floored. You were always pretty in school, but you grew up to be a beautiful woman, Britton."

"Thank you," Britton said. "I'm still a little shocked. I really wish you had talked to me back then instead of treating me like shit. We could have resolved a lot of things."

"I know. I need to thank you for keeping my secret safe for all of these years when you could have easily told everyone."

"As I said, it wasn't my secret to tell. Besides, I wasn't going to ruin it for myself. When you're a sophomore and a hot senior is naked in your bedroom and she kisses you, you sort of keep that to yourself," Britton shrugged. "I wanted more, you know."

"I did too." Daphne paused. "Still do," she said, peering over her glass as she took a sip of wine.

"Then why are you still an asshole towards me? We were kids back then."

"I guess in a way I was angry. You live this out and proud life without a care in the world and I hide in the closet, stupidly harboring feelings for you."

Britton stood to put some space between them and walked into the kitchen with her empty glass. She set the glass near the sink and leaned against the counter, looking out over the living room.

"You should have told me how you felt."

"You weren't exactly nice to me either, all of these years. I doubt that would have gone over well."

"I can't tell you either way. We shared a schoolgirl crush, but I was always attracted to you, Daphne. I still am, but I can't be an experiment."

Daphne stood and walked into the kitchen with her empty glass. Leaning around Britton, almost fully touching her body, she placed the glass near the sink. "You may have been the first girl I ever kissed, but you certainly weren't the last," she said before stepping away.

Britton grabbed her wrist, pulling Daphne against her and kissing her softly.

Daphne welcomed the kiss, taking the time to taste the woman who unknowingly took her breath away. She ran her hands up Britton's arms to her neck and into her thick hair before settling them on her chest just above her breasts. Britton wrapped her arms around Daphne's waist, tucking her thumbs under her shirt and rubbing along the soft skin of her lower back. She pressed her hips into Daphne's, pushing her back against the counter and sliding her tongue inside as Daphne's lips opened to her.

Realizing what she was doing, Britton paused, pulling away from the embrace to catch her breath. She looked back at the beautiful green eyes staring at her.

"We can't turn back time," Britton whispered.

"Britton, I stopped this once and it's haunted me for almost ten years. I'm not letting you go again," Daphne said, reaching out to her.

"What if this one night is all that I want?" Britton asked cautiously. Her mind raced in multiple directions, from confusion to nervousness to desire.

"I'm not asking for anything more," Daphne said, pressing her lips to Britton's once again. The aching in her chest was almost unbearable. She had dreamt of this very moment so many nights that she wasn't sure if it was real. She silently begged herself to not wake up if it wasn't.

Britton grabbed Daphne's hand and led her down the hall. Inside her bedroom, Britton reached around Daphne's back, unhooking her bra. Slowly, she pulled Daphne's shirt and bra over her head revealing her slender body and round breasts. Britton bent her head, snaking her tongue out and sucking a pink nipple between her lips. Moving her mouth along Daphne's body, she kissed her way up to her lips while unbuttoning her pants. Daphne ran her hands over Britton's stomach, feeling the taut muscles, before pulling her shirt over her head and tossing it behind her on the floor. She released the clasp on Britton's black satin bra and slid the straps down her arms.

Daphne tossed the bra on the floor, stepping back a half step to take in the body she remembered so well. Britton still carried the feminine, slightly muscular build of the athlete she once was. Her skin held a natural bronze complexion and was as silky smooth as it looked. Daphne reached up, sliding both palms over Britton's round perky breasts and dark nipples. Britton melted into the touch, moving closer until their bodies were pressed tightly together. She slid Daphne's pants down over her hips as they kissed again.

Daphne back away slightly to kick her pants off. Britton removed her jeans and both women tossed their panties into the pile of clothing on the floor.

"Are you sure you want to do this?" Britton gently asked, moving closer once more.

"I've never wanted anything more," Daphne said, peering into soft gray eyes.

Britton grabbed Daphne's hand and walked over to her bed. She pulled the thick comforter back, exposing dark satin sheets. Daphne moved onto the bed, on her back, with Britton crawling on top of her. Britton's long hair cascaded over her back and one of her shoulders as she leaned down, sucking a pink nipple into her mouth. She took her time, running her hand over Daphne's skin.

"Britton, I've waited almost ten years to feel your hands on me," Daphne said, breathlessly. "Don't make me wait any longer," she pleaded as she tried to calm her rapid breathing.

Britton grinned, sliding her hand up Daphne's leg to the wetness waiting at her center. Her own body tightened with arousal as she ran her fingers through the wet folds in lazy circles. Daphne's hips moving slowly with each pass until Britton pushed two fingers inside her. Daphne moaned and Britton kissed her passionately, sliding her fingers deeper and then almost all the way out with each stroke. Daphne's hips bucked under her and her short nails scrapped over the delicate skin of Britton's back.

Britton clearly knew what she was doing and was able to touch her like a lover without even knowing her.

"Oh, Britton, you feel so good," Daphne panted as her entire body went rigid, releasing the years of built up tension.

Britton kissed her softly while pulling her fingers free. Daphne tightened her arms around Britton, rolling her onto her back without breaking the kiss. Britton spread her legs and Daphne moved between them. Pressing her wetness against Britton's, she trailed tender kisses over her shoulder and along the edge of her neck, before moving back to her lips.

Britton's arousal had her teetering on the edge and Daphne knew it. She had obviously done this before. Daphne moved her hips back and forth over Britton's until Britton couldn't take it any longer. She grabbed Daphne's hand, forcing it between them.

Daphne smiled, sliding her fingers through the wetness, circling her over and over.

"Go inside me," Britton gasped.

Daphne pressed her lips to Britton's as she slid her fingers through her opening. Britton opened her legs further, allowing her to go deeper with each stroke. Daphne felt Britton tighten around her fingers.

Britton held her breath, seeing multiple colors flash before her eyes as she gave herself over to the adorable blonde on top of her. Daphne kissed her softly once more before moving alongside her. Britton wrapped her arms around Daphne and slowly caught her breath as her body began to relax.

~

Britton sat at her desk the next morning trying to work on her project, but the only visions behind her eyes were of Daphne's naked body. She grinned. They hadn't exactly made plans to see each other again and Britton wasn't sure she wanted to go down that road, especially after waking in the middle of the night with Daphne tucked up against her. No matter how attracted to her she was, or how many years she'd harbored that attraction, Daphne lived in the closet and Britton wasn't sure if getting involved with her was a good idea. Still, she let the images linger a little longer before forcing herself to get back to work.

Chapter Twelve

The longest workday in Britton's life was about to end. She watched the last hour click down on the clock. She finally finished the sketches for the law office building she was working on and planned to present them to the client first thing in the morning. She contemplated sneaking out a half-hour early when her phone beeped. She raised an eyebrow, checking the new text message.

Hey.

Britton laughed. The entire day had gone by with no word from Daphne, then all of a sudden a text that says 'hey'. She typed a quick message back.

Hello.

Britton had enough of sitting at her desk watching the clock, so she packed up her briefcase and headed towards the parking lot.

Are things going to be weird between us now? Daphne texted.

No. Britton texted back. *What the hell am I supposed to say?* She thought and texted again.
Is this a conversation u want to have over a text msg?

No.
I want to see you again.

I don't think that's a good idea, Britton texted. She wanted to see Daphne again, but the thought of dating her scared Britton.

This thing between us isn't going to be resolved in one night. U know that, right?

Britton parked her car in front of her apartment building. She sat in the car for a few minutes reading and rereading the latest message from Daphne. Sighing, she texted her back.

I'm home if you want to come by. I can't make any promises though.

Britton went inside and changed from her pantsuit to a comfortable pair of shorts and a T-shirt with nothing under it. She was about to scroll through her delivery menus when her phone rang.

"Hey, mom," she answered.

"Hello darling," her mother said. "Bridget mentioned that you planned to go to Wade's bachelor party this Friday night."

"Yes," Britton said.

"I really don't think that's a good idea."

"And why is that?"

"I know you went to Greg's party at that...that place and had a little too much to drink. I just don't think it's a respectable thing to do, Britton."

If you knew how many times I've been to the titty bar, Mom, you would keel over right where you stand. Britton thought, shaking her head. A knock on the door caught her attention.

"Mom, someone's at the door. I need to go."

"Well, do you know who it is? Don't just open your door for strangers."

"I have no idea who it is," Britton said, pulling the door open. Anyone, even a serial killer, would be better at this point than the awkward conversation she was having with her mother.

Daphne was standing in her doorway with a grin on her face, wearing a thin khaki-colored tank top that barely covered her naked breasts and showed a thin line of bare skin where it rose on her waist. Britton bit her bottom lip, quelling the desire she immediately felt building in her belly.

"Mom, I need to go. I'll call you tomorrow."

"Who's at your door, Britton?"

"Bye, Mom," Britton said, ending the call.

"Did you just hang up on your mom?" Daphne raised an eyebrow.

Britton nodded, pulling her inside. She closed the door, backing Daphne against it with her body as she kissed her soft lips. Britton traced her tongue over the edge of Daphne's mouth and nibbled on her lower lip, before kissing her deeply.

Daphne wrapped her arms around Britton's shoulders and Britton ran her hands under Daphne's shirt, feeling the smooth skin of her stomach and moving up to her breasts as she pushed the shirt up. Daphne's perky round breasts bounced slightly when they were released from the tightly stretched shirt. Britton broke the kiss and bent her head, sucking a pink nipple between her lips as she palmed the other breast, teasing the nipple between her finger and thumb.

Daphne moaned, rocking her hips, unknowingly searching for contact. Britton grinned, sucking the nipple harder as Daphne's hand moved through her hair holding her head to her breast. Britton moved her hands lower, opening Daphne's pants and pushing them down over her ass. They fell loosely to the floor in a mass of fabric as she tugged her panties down, adding them to the pile. Daphne moved her feet enough to step out of the clothing as Britton's mouth moved to assault her other breast.

Britton ran her fingers delicately through the wetness between Daphne's legs. Daphne's hips moved against her. Britton pulled her mouth away from Daphne's chest, kissing her lips while her fingers stroked her in lazy circles. Daphne's legs began to wobble, threatening to give out at any moment. She tightened her arms around Britton's shoulders for support.

Realizing she was basically naked and Britton was still fully dressed, Daphne ran her hands down Britton's chest over her breasts to the bottom of her shirt. She removed Britton's hands from her body long enough to pull the shirt over Britton's head, revealing her round breasts and dark nipples. Britton's shorts were the next thing to join the pile on the floor. Daphne's eyes were heavy with desire as she looked back at the woman in front of her.

Britton grabbed Daphne's hand and pulled her over to the couch, where she sat down. Daphne grinned and straddled her lap. She knew she was close as she kissed Britton, kneading both of her breasts and trying to prolong the impeding orgasm. Britton put one hand on the small of Daphne's back and slipped the other between them, easily entering her. Daphne arched her back with a low moan, breaking the kiss. Britton pushed her fingers deeper, while bending her head to take a nipple into her mouth, as Daphne's hips rocked back and forth, riding her.

Daphne pulled Britton's head up from her breast and kissed her hard. She slid her clit back and forth over Britton's palm while her fingers worked in and out of her. Britton ran her free hand up and down the soft skin of Daphne's bare back.

Britton felt the warm muscles tighten around her fingers as Daphne threw her head back with a guttural groan. The spasms continued as Daphne's body went limp, collapsing against her. She slipped her fingers free, holding the blonde as she caught her breath.

Seconds later, Daphne lifted her head from Britton's shoulder, kissing her tenderly, before sliding off her lap to the floor. Britton watched as Daphne ran her hands back and forth over her legs before pushing them apart at the knees. Daphne bent her head, placing warm kisses on Britton's stomach, working her way lower.

Britton slid her hips slightly forward on the couch, allowing Daphne better access as she dipped her head to taste. Britton threw her head back against the couch cushion when Daphne's tongue traced her swollen folds, dipping inside. She moved one hand to the blond head in her lap and interlaced the fingers of her other hand with Daphne's.

Daphne licked and sucked, alternating between hard and soft motions. Britton moaned, rocking her hips as much as she could in her position, trying desperately to keep up with Daphne's mouth. Her body tightened. She knew she was close, but the unexpected spasm tore through her body. Britton pushed Daphne's head away, panting and gasping as her body shivered.

Daphne watched in awe, unable to believe the last two days. Leaning forward, she ran her hand over Britton's cheek, teasing her lips with her thumb. *I'm falling for you all over again. It seems like I've wanted you all of my life. Please don't break my heart.*

Britton finally caught her breath, and opening her eyes, she saw Daphne staring back at her intently with a lazy grin on her face.

"You look lost in thought," Britton said softly.

"You're beautiful." Daphne smiled.

Britton grabbed her hands, tugging her up from the floor. Daphne sat down, cuddling up next to her and Britton pulled the afghan from the back of the couch, draping it over them.

"You were holding out on me last night," Britton teased.

"I was nervous. Besides, you held back, too."

"I wasn't sure how intimate you had been with another woman. I didn't want to freak you out. Clearly, I was mistaken." she laughed.

"Oh, I see. So you were waiting until the second or third date to whip out your huge strap-on?" Daphne tried to keep a straight face, but busted out laughing.

Britton rolled her eyes, laughing. "Heather loves to have a good laugh at my expense sometimes. She wanted to see the look on Leslie's face, but I noticed the look on yours instead."

"Really? And what look would that be?"

"I would describe it as sort of a deer in the headlights stare."

Both women laughed.

"For the record, I don't walk around with a strap-on under my pants. In fact, I don't really have any toys. I've been with women who were into that sort of thing and that's okay, but personally, I do just fine without them," Britton said.

"And here I was thinking how hot it would be to sneak into your office in the middle of the day to ride you while you sat at your desk," Daphne said, pretending to be disappointed.

Britton laughed. "Somehow, I don't see you as *that* girl."

"Good because I'd probably die of..." She paused when her stomach growled loudly. "I was going to say embarrassment, but apparently it's starvation."

"Don't you feed that thing?" Britton chuckled.

"Well, someone promised me the best delivery food in town last night and never followed through on her promise. I'm still holding out."

Britton shook her head. "I guess I better feed the beast," she joked and got up to call in their order.

Chapter Thirteen

The next evening, Britton and Daphne devoured multiple boxes of American Chinese food that Britton picked up on her way home, leaving empty containers all over the dining room table that was miraculously free of the piles of drawings that had adorned it the last two nights.

"Are we going to talk?" Daphne asked.

She was sitting across from Britton at the table and dressed in a borrowed T-shirt and shorts. Britton had also changed into shorts and a T-shirt when she got home from work.

"We've been talking for an hour."

"You know what I mean," Daphne said, seriously.

Britton sighed. "I don't know what you want me to say. You live in the closet, Daphne. I don't."

"I know. Hell, the whole state knows you're a lesbian."

Britton laughed. "I doubt that."

"I didn't mean you get around." Daphne grinned. "Although, you are pretty skilled."

"I could turn that right back around on you, you know."

"Easy, killer. Seriously though, when you came out your freshman year of high school you pretty much didn't care who knew or what they thought. As a star athlete your name was known around the state and you didn't exactly hide anything. It's fairly easy to put two and two together. As a matter of fact, a lot of people thought you and Heather were together."

"That was a decade ago and Heather and I? Really? That's just wrong. She's more of a sister to me than my own sister. People who thought that are stupid and obviously ignorant."

"To each her own." Daphne shrugged.

"Wait, did you think that?" Britton asked.

"Maybe, for a little bit, I guess," Daphne said.

"No wonder you were such a bitch to both of us," Britton said, shaking her head. "That explains a lot."

"Yeah, jealousy on top of being scared to death that you were going to out me didn't exactly make for civility where you were concerned."

"No kidding."

"Seriously, Britton, I want to see where this goes. I've carried these feelings for you for a long time and I know it's not a schoolgirl crush and it's not something a one night stand can extinguish."

Britton turned gray eyes on Daphne. "Why haven't you come out? I guess I don't understand."

"My family is nothing like yours or even Heather's for that matter. My mother would probably have a stroke.

She might be Heather's mom's sister, but they are two completely different peas from the same pod."

"You're almost twenty-seven. Do you expect to live the rest of your life hiding from your mother?"

Daphne huffed. "I don't know, Britton. I just...don't know."

"I care for you, Daphne, but I can't be your little secret."

"I care about you too." *More than you'll probably ever know*, she thought. "I'm not asking you to be. Can we just see where this goes? No one is saying we have to move in together or get married," Daphne said, reaching across the table for Britton's hand.

Britton squeezed the warm hand in hers. "As long as you understand I'm not hiding from who I am. I won't tell anyone I'm seeing you, until you're ready, but I'm also not going to wait forever."

"Do you want to come over to my place and stay tomorrow night? I'm a pretty good cook and from what I've seen of your take-out menu pile it looks like you don't cook."

"A cook, I am not," Britton grinned, doing her best Yoda impression. "I'd love to see where you live. It's in New Bedford, right?"

"Yeah, about thirty-five minutes from here, maybe forty with traffic."

"I bet you had the pick of the lesbian litter living in Massachusetts." Britton wiggled her eyebrows.

Daphne laughed. "Not exactly. I've dated a few girls over the past couple of years that I lived there. Nothing has been serious though. I haven't experienced having a 'Victoria'."

Britton cringed. "Trust me, you don't want to. That woman is crazy and not the good kind."

Daphne laughed. "I think I saw that first hand."

"I actually haven't been in a lot of serious relationships. I mean, I've dated, a lot, but I would say only two or three were serious enough to call my girlfriend."

"A lot? As in how many?"

Britton chuckled, shaking her head. "A woman doesn't kiss and tell how many notches are on her bedpost."

"Uh-huh."

"It's not as many as you think. I can assure you and I'm clean. I go to the lady doctor annually and get poked and prodded like any self-respecting lesbian."

Daphne laughed.

Britton's phone rang and she rolled her eyes, letting it go to voicemail. "I better call her back or she will think someone killed me."

"Why would she think that?"

"I was getting the third degree about going to Wade's bachelor party Friday, when you knocked on the door last night. I wouldn't tell her who was at the door and sort of hung up on her when I saw you standing there looking like sex on a stick."

"Nice analogy," Daphne laughed hysterically. "Wait, you haven't called her back since last night?"

"No. I was sort of preoccupied and then I had a busy day today."

Daphne laughed again.

Britton held her finger to Daphne's mouth as she waited for her mother to answer. Daphne sucked the finger into her mouth swirling her tongue around it.

Britton raised her eyebrows. "Hey, Mom," she said, snatching her finger away.

"Thank God. I was about to call the cops, Britton Marie."

"I'm sorry. I should've called you back."

"I called you three or four times last night."

"You did?" Britton didn't remember hearing her phone, but then again she was pleasantly distracted.

"Yes and I even called you today too."

"I must have my ringer turned down and I never got the message."

"Well, turn it up. I'm too old to worry about some stranger muscling their way into that apartment and hurting you."

"I'm fine, mom," Britton rolled her eyes.

"I talked to your father about this party and he agrees."

"Mom, we've been over this. I'm an adult and I'm going to the party. Trust me, I will not be drinking as much as I did at Greg's party. I don't even know where we are going. I seriously doubt Bridget is going to let Wade go to a topless club anyway."

"Oh good heavens, I hope not. Those places are so sleazy. I still cannot believe you went to one of them."

Britton sighed. "Again, I'm grown, Mom. I think I can make my own decisions."

"Sometimes, you don't make the best ones, as we've seen in the past. Your father is worried about you."

"Tell Daddy I'm fine. Now, I'm really busy working on a new project. I have to go. I'll talk to you soon. I love you," Britton said, finally getting off the phone.

"Is his party tomorrow night or next Friday?"

"Tomorrow night," Britton said. "Oh, shit. You want to make dinner. I guess I can cancel on Wade."

"That would make your mom happy."

"True, but I'd never hear the end of it if I let her win. Maybe I can come over afterwards or Saturday."

"Bridget's bachelorette party is Saturday," Daphne said.

"I know that. Maybe I can come over early and sneak back for the party later," Britton said, wiggling her eyebrows.

Daphne laughed. "So, you're going to stand me up to go to a titty bar and then come over for a booty call?"

Britton cringed. "Yeah, I guess it does sound like that, huh."

"Go to the party, Britton. You already said you were going. It's fine. I have a lot to do with Bridget's party anyway."

"Okay. Maybe we can plan to get together Sunday," Britton said.

"That sounds good. So, do your parents still give you shit about not going to work for your family's company?" Daphne asked. She'd overheard the conversation between Britton and her mother.

"Oh yeah, that and also giving up rowing to go draw and play with models. My mom usually doesn't say much, but my dad is pretty vocal about it. He hasn't been interested in my life in a long time. Making the Dean's List all of my bachelor's and master's degree years at MIT didn't even make him proud. He has an empty case that used to hang in his office at the house in Newport. It was for my Olympic medal. He finally took it off the wall two years ago."

"Wow. I had no idea he was so serious about all of that. I mean I knew he was pissed when you decided to go to MIT, but clearly you're brilliant and very talented at what you chose to do with your life. That model of the new building completely opened my eyes to a whole new side of you and those drawings in your bedroom took my breath away."

"Thanks. He doesn't see things the way you do, but that model did hit him pretty hard. He said a few things to me that suggest he's proud of me. I don't think he will ever get over me having nothing to do with the business."

"Yeah, that was an equally large shock. Everyone in this state assumed you would take the reins from your old man one day."

"It's never going to happen. So, if my family's money is what you're after you might as well give up or go after Bridget. I hold stock in the company, but she has the majority between the two of us and she will hold controlling interest when my father steps down or passes away."

"I can't believe you just said that, Britton. Do you really think I want you for the money?"

"No. I'm only teasing you. I'm serious though. Everything goes to Bridget."

"That's good because I don't want money. I want you for the eye candy. You're beautiful, Britton." Daphne smiled, running her hand over Britton's.

"Eye candy? You live in the closet. When and where are you going to parade around with me at your side?" Britton joked.

"I don't plan to always live in the closet."

"God, I hope not or this will be the shortest non one-night stand romance in history."

Daphne smacked her hand and smiled brightly. *I can't believe I wasted all of these years resenting you and adoring you at the same time. If I'd simply given in to my stupid pride who knows where we would be now,* Daphne thought.

"You look lost in thought," Britton said, her gray eyes studying Daphne's green ones.

"I was thinking about the way you tasted on my tongue," Daphne said, seductively.

"Oh, well, I can jog your memory if you like. The bedroom is right down the hall," Britton wiggled her eyebrows.

Standing up, she pulled Daphne to her feet, holding her in her arms. She still wasn't used to the feeling that came over her when she held Daphne. It was a mixed feeling of longing and desire, something she'd never really encountered with other lovers. It equally captivated and scared her.

Daphne threaded her arms around Britton's neck, leaning in for a simple kiss that heated quickly. Britton released the hold she had on Daphne and grabbed her hand, leading her down the hallway.

Chapter Fourteen

Britton walked into the *Pink Pony* and looked around the club as her eyes focused in the dim lighting.

"Can I help you?" a dancer nearby asked as she slinked her way up to Britton's side. She was wearing black fishnet stockings, a hot pink thong, black knee-high vinyl boots, and a black fishnet bikini top.

Britton eyed her attire and noted that the girl would actually be pretty if she wiped off the caked-on makeup and hadn't surgically enhanced her boobs to the point of floatation devices.

"I'm looking for my soon-to-be brother-in-law's bachelor party. His name is Wade," Britton said.

"Oh, yeah they're in the back. I'll show you," the girl said, turning and trotting off with her boots making a loud clacking noise on the floor as she walked.

Britton followed her into a small private room with a few couches and a pole in the center of the room. Wade was in a chair on the small platform with a small group of his friends occupying the couches.

"Hey, you made it," Wade called out. "This is my lesbian sister-in-law. Isn't she hot?" he said to the two dancers standing in the room.

Britton shook her head and laughed. "How much has he had?" she asked one of the guys.

"We started about an hour ago, so a lot."

"I see," Britton said.

She was barely seated in an open couch space when one of the dancers stood with her legs straddling Britton's.

"Would you like a dance?" the blond dancer asked, pushing her tits together and rubbing the nipples with her thumbs.

Britton had never been to the *Pink Pony*, but it was definitely different from the *Cat Box*. She politely shook her head no and pointed to the pole.

"I like to watch," she said with a grin.

The dancer took the hint and climbed up on the pole. Britton watched her swing around, twisting and gyrating to the thumping music.

~

An hour later, Britton had consumed two shots and hadn't let a single dancer touch her. She was having a good time, but sitting on a couch in the strip club wasn't where she wanted to be. She congratulated Wade and told his buddies to get him home safely because they wouldn't want to face the wrath of her sister. Then, she put the top down on her car and drove across state lines to a small row of six townhouses situated in a residential area. She squinted her eyes, trying to see the numbers in the dark. She finally just parked on the street since she wasn't sure which one was number 321. Getting out of her car, she pushed her hair over her shoulder and walked towards the narrow driveways. As many times as she had seen Daphne, she actually had no idea what she drove.

The third driveway had a small, two-door Mercedes in the driveway. Britton raised an eyebrow and decided to go check that one out first. The number above the door was 321. She grinned and knocked.

~

Daphne was sitting on the couch eating ice cream and watching Titanic for the thousandth time, but it didn't matter. She loved the story and Kate Winslet's boobs were definitely worth watching the movie over and over. Jack and Rose had just made love in the back of the old car. "That's definitely going on my bucket list. I wonder if Britton..." A loud knock on the door startled her from her daydream.

Daphne looked at the door, then at the clock on the wall and back at the door, wondering who was at her house at nine-thirty at night. She set her bowl of ice cream on the table and walked over to the door. Looking through the peephole, she saw nothing. Staying in the same spot, she reached blindly to the switch on the wall, turning the outside light on.

~

Britton stood on the doorstep waiting. She was just about to knock again when the bright light above her head came on, temporarily blinding her as if someone had

103

Graysen Morgen

just shone a flashlight in her eyes. She backed away, shading her eyes from the harsh light.

"Britton?" Daphne questioned, pulling the door open.

Britton smiled. "We have to stop meeting like this. People might start to talk," she said, leaning lazily against the door frame.

Daphne leaned against the door, smiling. "Oh really? And what would they say?"

"That you're madly in love with me." Britton grinned.

If you only knew, she thought. "Uh-huh. But, you're the one at my door in the middle of the night," Daphne teased.

Britton shrugged, smiling again. "There's no need for technicalities."

Daphne shook her head, smiling back. "How was the strip club?"

Britton rolled her eyes. "Fine, but it wasn't where I wanted to be," she murmured, stepping closer.

Daphne grabbed the lapels of her jacket, pulling her inside. Britton's lips met hers as the front door closed behind them. Britton kissed like she hadn't seen her in months instead of hours.

"Mmm, you taste like strawberries," Britton said, wrapping her arms around Daphne, kissing her again.

Daphne pulled away laughing and pointed at the bowl on the table. "I was eating ice cream."

Britton looked at the small living room. It was decorated in earth tones with a khaki colored couch and a brown recliner with brown throw pillows on the couch. The small dining room and kitchen was directly behind the living room and a narrow staircase was off to the side.

104

Britton looked up at the railing of a loft over the kitchen and dining room.

Following her eyes, Daphne said, "That's the bedroom. There is a half bath down here and a regular bathroom up there, but it doesn't have a tub, only a stand-up shower. It's small, but cozy."

"I like it. How long have you lived here?" Britton asked, still holding Daphne in her arms.

"I started renting this place when your father promoted me and transferred me to the distribution center here. It's been a little over two years now. This block of townhouses was here before the neighborhood went up around it. The owner wouldn't sell when the development moved in. He used to rent to various family members, but they've all moved on and bought houses so now this is just rental income for him. He and his wife are in their seventies and live in the light blue house across the street. They look out for me and call me the daughter they never had. They're really sweet. Their grandson handles all of the maintenance and lawn care. It's really quiet here. All of my neighbors are older. One old couple on the end has lived here for fifteen years."

"Wow. That's interesting."

A gunshot on the TV turned both of their attention to the flat screen. Britton raised an eyebrow.

"So, you sit on the couch eating ice cream and watching Titanic on a Friday night? That's exciting," Britton teased.

"It's better than sitting in a smoky bar watching skanky girls dance on men," Daphne shot back as she stepped out of Britton's embrace.

"Touché," Britton said. "I'm definitely where I want to be now. Ice cream and Titanic included."

Daphne laughed, carrying her bowl of melted ice cream soup to the kitchen. "You scared the hell out of me, you know," she chided, returning to the living room.

"You don't have a line of sexy hot women knocking on your door at night?" Britton sat down on the couch, eyeing Daphne's body from her silky smooth legs to her slender waist and past the natural curve of her round breasts to her adorable smile and striking green eyes.

Daphne felt Britton's eyes burning a path along her body. Tucking a loose strand of hair behind her ear and walking towards her, she said, "Yeah, as a matter of fact, you just missed the latest one."

"It's a good thing I'm not the jealous type then," Britton said, holding her arms out as Daphne sat on her, straddling her lap.

"Did you miss me?" Daphne asked huskily.

"I'm here aren't I?" Britton said, wrapping her arms around Daphne and pulling her forward. Their lips met in a passionate kiss.

~

A loud knock on the door the next morning brought Daphne out of the fog her mind was drifting in. She looked at the brunette sleeping nude next to her and smiled. The knock sounded again and Daphne jumped up, realizing the knocking on the door was what woke her up. The clock on the nightstand had the numbers nine, three, and two lit up in bright red LED.

How the hell did I sleep past 9:30? And who the hell is knocking on my door?

Daphne pulled on a pair of shorts and a T-shirt over her naked body and padded down the stairs. She looked through the peephole and froze.

"Fuck!" she whispered loudly and ran back up the stairs.

"Britton! Wake up!" she hissed, shaking the sleeping woman.

Britton shooed her away.

"Seriously! Britton! You have to get up now!" she said loudly in her ear.

"What?!" Britton opened her eyes, rolling over.

The knock on the door echoed again. Britton looked towards the rail that overlooked the living area.

"Your sister is at my front door," Daphne growled.

"Let her knock."

"My car is in the drive way and she has a key!" Daphne growled again.

"Oh, shit!"

"No kidding. You need to hide...NOW!" Daphne jumped off the bed, rushing down the stairs.

Britton collected her clothes and shoes and squeezed into the closet, still naked as Daphne pulled the front door open.

"What took you so long? I was about to use my key," Bridget said, walking inside.

"I stayed up late watching a movie and I must have slept in. I haven't even had my coffee yet," Daphne replied.

"I brought you one." Bridget handed her best friend a vanilla latte.

"Oh, you're a God," Daphne said, taking a long swallow.

~

The creamy scent of the coffee made its way upstairs. Britton craned her neck to smell the aroma and hear what they were saying and leaned too far, bumping her head on the closet door.

Ouch! Shit! Fuck you, Bridget!

~

"What was that?" Bridget looked towards the loft, making a move to go up there.

"Shit," Daphne whispered.

"Huh?"

"Rat. There's a rat in the attic," Daphne said.

Bridget cringed. "Gross. It sounds big."

"Yeah." *A naked and probably pissed off, five foot seven inch, one hundred and thirty-five pound, sexy as hell, rat.*

"Did your landlord put out traps?"

"Uh...yeah. Yeah he did it last week. That might have been one of the traps. I should probably get him over here and get that taken care of before the party this afternoon," Daphne said, ushering Bridget back to the door.

"I stopped by because I was at the dress shop this morning, picking up my mother's dress for her and they told me you hadn't picked up your shoes. I brought them to you," Bridget said, pointing to the bag on the floor that Daphne hadn't noticed.

"Oh, that's great. I've been pretty busy this week." *Damn it. I completely forgot to go get those.*

"My dad knows you've been preoccupied with all of this wedding stuff. Is he working you too hard?"

No, your sister is, she thought. "No...it's just been a chaotic week. Thanks for the shoes and the coffee. I better get on the phone with Jimmy so he can get that rodent out of my closet."

"I thought it was in your attic?"

"It is."

"You just said closet," Bridget raised an eyebrow.

Daphne laughed nervously and sipped the coffee. "I'm a mess without my coffee in the morning. I'll see you this afternoon."

"Alright. Oh hey, you haven't by chance seen my sister, have you?"

"Your sister? No. Why would I be seeing your sister?"

"That looks like her car parked on the street."

"She sure as hell isn't here."

Bridget laughed. "Yeah, I didn't think so. Must be someone else around here with a need for speed," she said, stepping through the doorway. "I'll see you in a few hours."

"Be ready to party hard," Daphne called out as Bridget walked to her car. She turned around smiling and waved as she got into her BMW.

"Holy fuck!" Daphne huffed, leaning with her back against the closed door. She blew out a deep breath and turned to check the peephole. Daphne's car was gone. "You can come out now!" she yelled.

Daphne heard rustling in the closet and walked up the stairs in time to see Britton's naked body emerge.

"I'm sorry," Daphne said, smiling.

Britton yawned, holding her hand out for the coffee cup, which Daphne relinquished without hesitation. She drank two long swallows, nearly draining the medium-sized cup.

"Rat?" she said, eyeing Daphne.

"I didn't know what to say. You were making noise." Daphne shrugged.

"I smacked my damn head on the door."

Daphne laughed and rose on her tippy toes, kissing Britton's forehead. "You're trouble, you know that?" she teased.

"How so?" Britton asked, wrapping her arms around Daphne, pulling the blonde against her.

"You show up at my door in the middle of the night. I have to hide you in my closet when someone comes over. You're my best friend's sister. Oh and did I mention my boss's daughter?" Daphne shook her head. "I'm asking for it."

Britton shrugged. "That doesn't sound like trouble to me."

"Really? What does it sound like then?"

Britton walked Daphne backwards. Pushing her softly back onto the bed, she crawled on top of her. "It sounds like you have a dirty little secret," Britton said seductively before claiming her lips in a heated kiss.

~

An hour and half later, Daphne kicked Britton out of her bed and out of her townhouse. It was already noon and her day hadn't even begun. She was drained from spending all night and all morning in bed with Britton. She still needed to get herself ready and get over to the country club and freshen the place up, decorate it, and pick up the food. All without getting sweaty or dirty since she was a half hour from home. The guests were arriving in four hours for the bridal shower and then the bachelorette party started afterwards, so she was in for a long night and all she wanted to do was go back to sleep.

Chapter Fifteen

Britton texted Daphne as she was heading out her door for the party.

Are you as tired as I am?

You have no idea. I've been running around like crazy since you left. All I want to do is put my feet up with a glass of wine and fall asleep in front of the TV. **Daphne texted back.**

You better get your 2nd wind. You have a house full of people coming over.

No I don't. Didn't you read your invitation?

Opps. I guess I was still arrogantly ignoring you and anything about you. I'm glad I haven't left yet. **Britton texted, searching for the invitation.**

LOL it's at the country club in the grand reserve room. Don't be late.

I actually planned on being fashionably late on purpose.

Why? **Daphne asked.**

You and I are supposed to hate each other. What better way to piss you off than to be late?

True.

Will you be able to pretend to hate my guts after you were begging me to go inside you only a few hours ago??? **Britton answered.**

Britton! LOL I guess I will have to try very hard.

After your little display of nerves this morning you better figure it out or you're going to look like the cat that ate the canary.

LOL you're probably right. I guess you better stay away from me all night. **Daphne texted.**

I had already planned that. Don't worry. Everything will be fine. Just pretend to treat me like shit and no one will know the difference.

You make it sound like that's okay. **Daphne typed.**

It has to be, unless you plan on sashaying out of the closet tonight. **Britton wrote back.**

LOL Not likely.

I'll see you in a little while. Remember to keep your hands to yourself and make snide comments about everything I say and do. :)

~

True to her word, Britton showed up just before the bride-to-be was set to arrive. She was wearing light gray pants, a lilac purple, sleeveless, button-down blouse, and black, backless sandals with a low heel. Her hair fell over her shoulders in loose waves as she walked over to the gift table to deposit the small bag she was carrying.

"It's about time you arrived," Sharon Prescott chided her daughter from nearby.

"I'm not late," Britton said to her mother as she looked around at the room. It was tastefully decorated with white and silver embellished candles, yellow roses, and a champagne fountain, which Britton made a beeline for.

"I thought maybe you would do me the honor of not showing up at all," Daphne sneered when Britton walked past her.

Britton turned, eyeing the beige, satin blouse and white pants Daphne was wearing. She winked and grinned before moving towards the rest of the group.

Bridget arrived minutes later and the party kicked off. Britton stayed on the opposite side of the room as the small crowd mingled around the food tables and sat down for the opening of gifts. Britton had just gotten up to refill her champagne glass when her sister opened her gift.

"Oh, Britton, this is beautiful," Bridget squealed.

Daphne turned to see Bridget holding up a beautiful platinum cross at least six inches long with gorgeous etching down the center and Bridget and Wade's names on one side of the cross bar and their wedding date on the opposite side.

Britton smiled at her sister.

"Oh, my. That's just like the one my parents were given when they were married," Sharon said from her seat next to Bridget. "It's hanging on the wall in my bedroom."

"I know. I've always admired it. Thank you so much, Britton."

"You're welcome. Now you don't have to wait for mom to give you grandma's. You have your own," Britton said, watching Daphne smile at her from her position next to Bridget on the opposite side of her mother.

The bridal shower finally wound down and half of the women left. The rest of the partygoers enjoyed a tray of white petit fours with yellow icing flowers on them and of course the remaining champagne still flowing through the fountain.

"That's going to go right to your ass," Britton said, watching Daphne eat the delicate dessert.

Daphne rolled her eyes, smiling as she walked away from her.

"Well, now that adults are gone, I think it's time to have a little bachelorette fun," Daphne said.

Moving to the center of the room with a chair, she called Bridget over and had her sit down. Then, she blindfolded her with a silk scarf and had everyone take seats in a circle around her.

"Alright, now each of us is going to go up and whisper to her something you did on your wedding night or plan to do, but you can't tell anyone else your secret and she can't repeat your secrets," Daphne said, pointing at one of the women to begin.

Britton sat back in her chair with her arms crossed thinking this was by far the dumbest thing she had ever seen, until she saw a man enter the room from the side. He had sun-tanned skin, toned muscles, and short, dark hair. Britton thought he looked vaguely familiar. The circle was just about to her and Britton had no idea what the hell she was going to tell her sister as her dirty little secret and she was sure whatever it was it would make her hair stand on end.

Britton watched as the guy opened the pants of his novelty cowboy costume and walked over to Bridget. He leaned down and whispered in her ear as he placed her hand inside his pants. Bridget shrieked and jumped, snatching the blindfold off. Everyone laughed and Daphne started the music on his portable player. He began a sultry, seductive dance as his costume

116

disappeared, piece by piece, until he was wearing only a thin G-string.

The guy spent the next hour dancing all over Bridget multiple times, as well as a few of the other women. When the guy approached Britton, she finally realized where she knew him from. She gladly let him straddle her lap. He moved to the music sliding his stiffness up and down her thigh.

"I thought that was you," he whispered in her ear.

She grabbed his bare ass cheeks with both hands pulling him harder into her. The women in the room cheered as he ground his pelvis hard into Britton's as the beat of the song picked up. Bridget and Daphne sat with their mouths hanging open in shock.

Britton ran her hands over his muscled body as the song slowed. He stilled his hips, kissed her tenderly on the mouth, and smiled brightly when the song ended. She wrapped her arms around him, hugging him tightly.

When he backed away to move to the next girl, Bridget appeared at Britton's side with Daphne moving to within earshot.

"Care to explain yourself?" Bridget asked. "Since when so you dry-hump half-naked men and let them kiss you?"

Britton laughed. "That's Erik. He's Victoria's little brother. I haven't seen him in at least a year. I forgot he was a dancer."

"It looked like you were pretty close."

"He's gay, Bridget."

"No way."

"Yes he is. I swear to you. He has a boyfriend named Javier."

Daphne stood rooted to the floor as Britton called Erik back over to her.

"Erik, this is my sister, Bridget."

"It's nice to meet you. Congratulations by the way," he said.

"How do you know my sister?" Bridget asked.

"She used to date my arrogant sister," he said, smiling.

"How's Javier?" Britton asked.

Erik's face lit up. "He's good. He's in New York visiting his parents this weekend. We should get together when he gets back. He just finished a new project and I know he would love to show it to you."

"That's great. Give me a call," she said, turning to her sister. "Javier is an interior designer. I've gotten him a few jobs through my firm."

"I see," Bridget said.

Erik walked over to Daphne, who refused a dance, pointing him to the small group of waiting women next to her. Bridget walked over to the champagne fountain and Daphne headed in her direction, but made a beeline for the bathroom when she saw Britton disappear around the corner.

Britton walked up to the mirror and shook her hair off her shoulders. She smiled when she saw Daphne walk up behind her.

"What was that little display? Care to explain yourself?" Daphne stood a foot away with a thin smile and a raised eyebrow.

"Did it turn you on?"

"Gross!"

Britton reached out to Daphne, pulling her close as she backed up against the sink. Daphne wrapped her arms loosely around Britton's neck. Leaning in, she pressed her lips softly to Britton's at first, then kissing her with wild abandon. Britton ran her hands from Daphne's slender waist to her tight ass, squeezing her cheeks and rocking her hips against Daphne's.

Realizing where they were, both women backed away from the heated exchange, grinning sheepishly at each other.

"God," Daphne said, tucking a loose strand of hair behind her ear as she waited for her racing heart to slow its pace.

"Yes," Britton answered confidently.

Daphne laughed. Shaking her head, she said, "You're trouble."

"So you've said." Britton grinned seductively.

"You're insufferable. Get out of here before someone comes in and craps on that ego of yours," Daphne teased.

Britton grinned and rolled her eyes, before leaving the room. Bridget was just about to walk in at the same time and they almost collided.

"Whoa," Bridget said.

"Sorry," Britton replied, storming off.

Bridget saw Daphne at the sink washing her hands.

"What's going on?" Bridget said.

"What do you mean?" Daphne asked.

"My sister just about mowed me down with the door as she stormed out of here."

Daphne shrugged. "I don't know. She's being her typically bitchy self. I asked her if she really was a lesbian because it looks like she and the stripper are hooking up. She told me to kiss her ass and she walked away."

Bridget laughed. "He's her ex-girlfriend's brother and apparently he's gay with a partner that she also knows."

"No way."

"Yeah, I'm serious."

"They still looked a little close if you ask me."

Bridget shrugged. "I don't get involved in Britton's sex life. It's way too complicated for me," she said, going into one of the stalls.

The party finally dwindled down after the stripper left, leaving Daphne and a few other people behind to clean up. Bridget offered to stay and help, but Daphne sent her home. Britton stayed to help since she was part of the wedding party, however, she managed to keep her distance from Daphne.

Britton went outside, walking around the building to see the golf course under the moonlight. She turned around when she heard the faint click of heels on the pavement.

"Everyone's gone," Daphne said. Standing next to her, she watched Britton looking out at the darkened course.

"I had a good time. The party was nice," Britton said.

"Thanks. I think your sister was happy," Daphne said, watching Britton staring into the distance with a lost look in her eyes. "What are you looking at?" she quietly asked.

"I had sex for the first time out there on the back nine. I was fourteen and her name was Maddy. She was here with her family for the annual Prescott's company Christmas party."

"Wow, and here I thought I was the first girl you ever kissed," Daphne said, smiling casually. "What made you think of that?"

120

Britton studied the dark spots in the moon. "I think of her every time I come here," Britton sighed. "She died of cancer the following summer. I never even knew she was sick."

"Oh my God, Britton. I'm sorry."

"I was just a kid, but my life changed that night."

"Thank you for sharing that with me," Daphne whispered.

Britton turned slightly, looking into her weary green eyes. "You look tired," she murmured.

"I'm exhausted." Daphne yawned.

"You should get some sleep."

"Do you want to come home with me?" Daphne asked.

Britton closed the distance between them, kissing her lips softly.

"Only if you promise to sleep. I know you're worn out and I'm having a family brunch with my parents and Wade and Bridget at the Newport house in the morning. I probably shouldn't show up looking like a sleep-deprived zombie," she said, smiling thinly.

"Scout's honor," Daphne grinned, interlacing her fingers with Britton's.

~

The next morning, Britton rolled over in her sleep, hearing a faint beeping sound. Prying her eyes open, she searched the unfamiliar room.

"Turn your phone off," Daphne growled, pulling the covers over her head.

Britton slid out of bed, tripping over shoes and clothes strewn around the floor as she made her way to

121

the stairs. She walked down to the living room where her phone was sitting on the kitchen counter, steadily beeping her morning alarm, announcing that it was eight o'clock. She turned the noisy device off and poured herself a glass of water.

The cold water did nothing to chase away the sleepiness in Britton. She craved a cup of coffee as bad as a smoker craved the first cigarette of the day. Yawning, she grabbed her phone and pushed a speed dial number.

"Hello?" Sharon Prescott answered vibrantly.

Britton cringed. Her mother was way too cheery for her own good. "Hey mom, I'm not going to make it to brunch. I'm not feeling very well," Britton said.

"Oh, what's wrong? Did you need me to bring you anything?"

"No. I'm fine. I stopped at a fast food place on the way home from the party last night. I guess it didn't sit well. I was up all night."

"My goodness," she sighed. "You shouldn't eat that kind of food, Britton. It will kill you."

"I know. I learned my lesson," Britton said.

She knew her mother was disappointed and overdramatic, but hosting one family meal without both of her children wouldn't kill her.

"Tell Daddy I love him and I will see you both at the rehearsal dinner Friday," Britton said, before hanging up. She set the phone back on the counter and padded back upstairs.

"You're going to hell," Daphne said without opening her eyes.

Britton lifted the covers and crawled on top of her. "Why is that?"

"You just lied to your mom."

Britton shrugged. "It's not the first time and probably not the last. Besides, I really was up all night. I should have remembered you weren't a scout. Technically, you're probably going to hell. You used treachery to get me in your bed and keep me awake for hours on end."

Daphne laughed, looking up at gray eyes staring down at her. "Your mother is going to hate me when she finds out I'm the reason you've been blowing her off," she said, wrapping her arms around Britton, running her hands up and down her back.

"Nah, she loves you. In fact, I'm surprised you weren't invited to that stupid family brunch too. She'd probably rather have you there than me," Britton said, kissing her lips.

"Oh that's not true and you know it," Daphne said.

"Are we really going to lie here and discuss my mom?" Britton raised an eyebrow and moved her hips against Daphne's.

Chapter Sixteen

Britton hated to see Monday and Tuesday come and go. She was happy to have her latest client proposal behind her, but they still had not contacted her about the changes she submitted to them. Getting the build for her father's business was great, but she needed to bring in other builds as well if she wanted to be offered a permanent position with the firm at the end of her one year internship contract. She had only three months left and the stress was starting to claw at her back.

She turned off the light at her drawing table and grabbed her keys from her desk drawer. She was already running late and needed to make a quick stop on her way to meet Heather for lunch.

~

"I'm going to start leaving for lunch a half hour later since noon to you is more like noon-thirty," Heather joked as her best friend sat down across from her.

Britton laughed. "I'm sorry. I had to run over to the family lawyer's office. Bridget and Wade are getting their marriage license today and I had to witness the signing of the prenup. She's driving me crazy."

"You sound like Daphne," Heather said. "Bridget's driving her crazy too."

"Yeah, I know it," Britton said, studying the menu. She hadn't seen Daphne since she left her house on Sunday afternoon.

Heather peered at her friend with a raised eyebrow.

"Bridget's driving everyone crazy. Her wedding is a few days away and she's acting a like a wet cat. I'm sure she's making Daphne run around like a headless chicken." Britton shrugged. "They're two peas in a pod and as far as I'm concerned they belong in each other's craziness."

"You look tired," Heather said, watching her best friend. "I don't think I've talked to you three times in the past two weeks."

"I know. I've been working like a dog. My contract is up soon and I'm trying to generate as much business as I can so I can keep my job."

"Do you think they will let you go?"

"I hope not," Britton said, pausing to give the waiter her order. "I really have no idea. There is no set amount of buildings or business dollars in my contract. I guess I could fight it if they fired me. I have two builds under my name and I assisted on another two. I'm really close to closing another one so that will give me three. That's actually a lot more than most people do during an unpaid internship, so they are getting what they wanted when they decided to give me a paid contract for one year."

"That's good then."

"Yeah," Britton said.

She hated lying to her best friend and in all actuality, she wasn't really lying. Her job was on the line and she had been stressed over it, but she'd been too busy with Daphne the past few weeks to think about anything or anyone else.

"I promise not to turn into a bridezilla on you next week," Heather joked.

"That's good because I'd have to smack you and tell you to calm your ass down."

"See, that's what I have you for, to keep me in line," Heather said. "Hey, how was Bridget's bachelorette party?"

"Fine. Daphne unknowingly hired Erik Reitz to strip at the party."

"Isn't that Victoria's brother?"

"Yes." Britton laughed. "He's a private party stripper. He was a hit. He must have walked away with five hundred dollars in tips."

"I bet that was a lot of fun."

"Oh yeah, everyone passed him around for about two hours."

Heather laughed. "My mom asked if you were bringing a date to the wedding. She's finishing the seating chart for the reception and you will be at the wedding party table, but she wanted to make sure your date had a seat. I told her you weren't seeing anyone, but I thought I'd ask just in case."

"No. I'll be with me and only me. Besides, who the hell would I take? I can't ask some random girl if she wants to go to a wedding with me and then say 'oh by the way, I'm in the wedding so you will have to sit at a table with strangers.' I'm sure that would go over really well," Britton said, laughing.

Heather shrugged. "That's true. At least you didn't say you were bringing Victoria."

"Hell no. That is definitely over," Britton said. Her stomach rumbled loudly as the waiter set their food in front of them.

~

Britton was sitting on her couch with her sketch pad in her lap, watching a documentary about Italian Renaissance. The TV was paused on the Rialto Bridge in Venice. She had no idea why the structure had captured her attention, but she began sketching the famous bridge.

She was halfway through the initial outline when her cell phone rang. Reluctantly, she answered her phone, ignoring the caller ID as she continued to sketch the lines of the bridge.

"Hello?" Britton said with a hint of annoyance in her voice.

"What are you doing?" Daphne asked.

Britton set the sketch pad on the couch next to her. "Drawing something on TV."

"Nerd," Daphne sighed. "I guess I'll let you go if you're busy."

"Wait, what did you want?"

"Do you miss me?" Daphne asked.

"That goes without saying. Do you miss me?"

"I wouldn't be calling you if I didn't."

"I bet you're ready to strangle my sister."

"That's an understatement," Daphne huffed.

"It'll all be over soon."

"Do you want to see me?" Daphne asked. "Or are you too busy drawing the TV?"

"I'm not drawing the TV," Britton laughed. "I'm drawing something on a documentary on the TV."

"Open your door," Daphne said.

Britton jumped off the couch, hurrying across the room. She was surprised to see Daphne standing there when she pulled the door open.

"Hi," Daphne said.

"Hi yourself." Britton smiled. "Get in here," she said. Pulling Daphne inside, she wasted no time as she backed her up against the door, kissing her as if her life depended on it.

"I guess you did miss me," Daphne mumbled between kisses.

"Nah," Britton teased. "I'm just horny and my vibrator batteries died."

Daphne's face distorted in shock, before growing into a large smile. "I guess we have to rectify that situation," she said.

"I guess so," Britton agreed, pulling Daphne away from the door and down the hall. The TV and sketchpad were long forgotten.

~

The next evening, Britton walked into the private dining room, casually late, but with a couple of minutes to spare.

"It's about time you showed up," Daphne hissed under her breath as Britton sat down next to her.

"Seriously?" Britton glared at her. "Why the hell did they seat me next to you?"

"Ladies?" Sharon Prescott scolded. "Britton, we've been waiting for you."

128

"Traffic was a mess," Britton lied. She'd actually been busy texting Daphne and lost track of time. She met Daphne's eyes, giving her a stern look. Daphne grinned and looked away.

The meal's four courses had been ordered ahead of time for the group and the first course arrived at the table quickly. Britton tore into her salad and tuned out her surroundings as the wedding planner went through the events of the following day.

"You better pay attention," Daphne whispered.

"Why? That's what you're for, to bitch at me and keep me in line," Britton whispered between bites.

She was starving. She'd worked through lunch because she planned to leave work early, but that backfired on her when she realized it was after six and she needed to be across town by six-thirty. She'd arrived at six-twenty-eight.

~

The rehearsal ended two hours later and Britton said goodbye to her family. She hated not seeing Daphne, but in true maid of honor fashion, she was hosting the bride for the evening. They had numerous appointments scheduled the next day, starting with their hair and nails first thing in the morning. Britton laughed at the thought of Daphne getting her nails done. She kept them very short, blaming her multiple hours on a computer as the reason, but Britton knew the truth.

Britton was headed home when she decided to make a quick detour. She pulled into the driveway of a small cottage style house and dialed a number on her phone.

"Hey," Heather said. "Is the dreaded dinner finally over?"

"Yep, what are you doing?" Britton asked.

"Sitting on my ass, drinking a glass of wine."

"Where's Greg?"

"He went to a poker game at a friend's house. I was invited, but that's not really my thing. Why? What's up?"

"Get dressed, I'm in your driveway."

"You are?" Heather walked over to the window, peering through the curtains.

Britton reached her hand through the open top, waving.

"Where are we going?" Heather asked.

"I don't know."

"Don't you have to be up and at it early tomorrow morning?"

"Nope. I don't have to do anything, except show up at my parent's house at noon ready to get my hideous dress on. Daphne's babysitting Bridget tonight and all day tomorrow."

"Nice," Heather said. "Come in for a minute. I need to throw some clothes on."

~

Britton was thrilled to be out with her best friend. She really hadn't seen her much lately and most of that was due to her sneaking around to see Daphne. She felt bad and hoped her friend wouldn't hate her when she found out. Some things were just unexplainable and better left unsaid, at least for the time being. When the time was right, she was sure everyone would welcome her new relationship with open arms. Anything had to be better than Victoria. Britton couldn't think of a single person who had been excited about that relationship, including herself.

Britton and Heather wound up at the new wine bar downtown where a blues band was playing. Together, they polished off two bottles of wine and danced until their feet hurt. Britton couldn't remember the last time she'd had so much fun with Heather. She actually missed all of the crazy fun things they used to do on the spur of the moment before relationships and work settled into their lives.

It was after two in the morning when Britton dropped Heather off. She offered her the tiny spare bed, but Britton chose to drive home to her own bed instead.

Chapter Seventeen

Britton woke up the next morning thankful she didn't have a hangover. She spent the morning relaxing on her couch with her feet up and a cup of coffee in her hand. She couldn't remember the last time she'd been able to just lounge around.

Later, she swung by the local salon for a quick trim and was showered and ready to go with a half-hour to spare when her phone beeped. She laughed when she saw the text message from Daphne.

Your mother and sister are making me crazy. What time r u going to be here???

I don't know if I can help. You're supposed to hate my guts. Remember? **Britton texted back.**

I'm at the point of hating all 3 of u at this moment. **Daphne quickly replied.**

I'm leaving now anyway. See u soon. Don't kill my family until I get there.

~

Britton arrived at her parent's estate house in Newport. She parked her car around the back near the garage instead of the long circular drive where the guests were parking. She noticed the large archway overlooking the bay down below with rows and rows of chairs behind it and a white aisle runner down the middle. A huge white tent was off to the side, in the process of being decorated for the reception.

Britton took a deep breath and went into the house through the side door. The kitchen was huge and bustling with the catering staff. The house had two living rooms and a den that she walked through, looking for any of her family members. Britton saw her father in his study when she walked by. He was drinking coffee at his desk with his laptop running in front of him.

"Hey, daddy," she said, poking her head in.

"Hey, darling," he replied, waving her in. "Are you ready for today?"

"Between this weekend and next, I'm ready to get this entire month over with."

"I hear you," he agreed, scrolling through an email.

"Craven told me yesterday that he's received the permits from the city. I forgot to tell you last night with all of the haste. We will probably set up a meeting this coming week to tie everything together. It looks like we are set to break ground on the first as planned," she said.

"That's great news. I'll have Rebecca call you Monday to set that up," he said, referring to his assistant.

"Good." She walked around his desk to give him and hug and a kiss. "I better get upstairs."

"Good luck," he said, smiling at her.

Britton walked back through the formal living room and up the grand staircase. She stopped at the first room in the hallway, which used to be her favorite room when she was a kid. She stayed in it when her family came to the Newport house on the weekends or to visit her grandparents when they lived there. She walked into the room and looked around. The walls were painted light blue and the entire room was decorated with nautical designs and pictures. The queen-sized bedding was a mixture of dark and light blue colors.

She checked herself in the mirror over the dresser one last time. *Here we go*, she thought as she headed further down the hall to the room that used to be her sister's favorite. It was also the room Daphne planned to spend the night in. Britton gave a light knock and walked into the room. It was a brightly lit room with faint yellow walls, white furniture and a sunflower bedspread on the queen-sized bed.

"It's about time you got here," Daphne sneered.

"It's lovely to see you too," Britton growled back.

"Don't even start you two," Bridget scolded.

Britton looked around at the room. Bridget's white dress was hanging on an old-fashioned wooden dress stand and Britton and Daphne's dresses were hanging on the back of the closet door.

"We need to get her dressed first, then we can get dressed," Daphne said to Britton.

"Why are we getting dressed so early?" Britton asked, checking the clock on the wall.

"The guests will start arriving in two hours. That's why!" Daphne snapped.

Britton rolled her eyes. "What do you need me to do?"

"She has to put on stockings, a corset, a garter, her shoes, the last touch of her makeup, the dress, her jewelry and the veil. In that order," Daphne grumbled.

"If you ladies have this, I need to go check with the caterer and the wedding planner," Sharon said.

"Yeah, we've got this, mom," Britton said, ushering her mother out of the room.

"What the hell did you do that for?" Bridget asked.

"Because, there's too damn much estrogen in this room. Everyone needs to chill out, take some nerve pills, drink some shots or hell, do a mixture of both."

"Britton!" her sister hissed in shock.

"Oh, lighten up. I didn't say smoke a joint, damn," Britton said.

Daphne tried not to laugh. She was having a difficult time keeping a straight face.

"What are you waiting on?" Britton looked at Daphne. "Let's do this. I'm assuming you know how to put your damn pantyhose on," she said to her sister.

Bridget nodded and took her robe off, revealing her naked body as she began pulling the sheer nylon hose up her leg. Britton turned away, fidgeting with the jewelry on the dresser.

"Son of a bitch!" Bridget shrieked.

Britton turned to see a huge run up the side of the stocking.

"I can't do this. I'm too nervous," Bridget growled, snatching the pantyhose off.

"Here," Daphne said, moving closer as she started another pair of pantyhose on her legs. "This is why we bought a bunch of pairs, Hon."

"I'm not wearing those things. That is where I draw the line on my femininity," Britton said. "Be glad she's here because I don't even know how to put the damn things on."

Bridget laughed. "I could only imagine if I was left with a lesbian to get me ready for my wedding," she said jokingly.

At that exact moment, Daphne ran her thumb right through the side of the pantyhose, making a huge hole. Britton laughed hysterically.

"Fuck!" Daphne said, rolling her eyes at Britton.

"The hell with it. I don't need the damn things," Bridget said.

"It's tradition. Come on, we'll try another pair. Maybe the lesbian giggle box over there wants to give it a try," Daphne chided.

"I already told you. I have no idea how to put those things on," Britton said. "I barely know how to get them off," she whispered.

Daphne shook her head.

"Oh, shut your mouth and give it a damn try. We're going to be here all day at step one," Bridget yelled.

Between the three of them they were finally able to get the pantyhose on without tearing anymore runs, followed by the corset and the garter, which were both slightly easier. Britton kept an eye on the clock as Daphne bent down, buckling the straps on Bridget's satin heels with mock diamonds. They had less than one hour to finish everything else on Bridget and then about thirty-minutes to get dressed themselves.

Bridget wanted to do her own makeup, which was perfectly fine with Britton since she'd never worn makeup a day in her life. Daphne wasn't a big makeup wearer either, so she was happy to relinquish one task from her list. As Bridget went to work on her face paint, Britton and Daphne set their dresses and accessories out.

"We need to get your dress on, Hon," Daphne said to Bridget as she watched her finish her makeup.

"Okay, I'm ready. At least it doesn't go over my head," Bridget joked nervously.

Daphne moved the dress to the center of the room and unzipped the back. Then she pooled the dress in a huge circle.

"You need to step in very carefully," she said to Bridget. "Britton, hold that side so that she doesn't step on it and then pull it up carefully."

Britton nodded, grabbing the dress with one hand and helping to steady her wobbly sister with the other. Once Bridget was in the center of the circle, Britton and Daphne pulled the dress up around her. Britton held it in place as Daphne zipped it up.

"Wow, you look amazing," Daphne said, fluffing the dress out around her waist.

"You do look really pretty, Bridge, but how the hell are you going to get down the stairs in that poufy thing?" Britton said.

"That's what she has us for, dipshit," Daphne scolded.

Britton shot her a menacing look with a raised eyebrow. Daphne smiled, shaking her head.

"Britton, you put her jewelry on and I'll get her veil," Daphne said, handing Britton a tray of jewelry pieces.

"Oh, I remember this. It was Grandma's," Britton said, putting the necklace around her neck. The heart shaped diamond pendant settled a few inches above her cleavage.

Bridget reached up, smiling as she touched it.

Britton went to work putting the small diamond and pearl hoop earrings in her ears and the matching tennis bracelet on her right wrist.

"That's it," Britton said.

Bridget's long hair was wrapped into a tight bun at the back of her head and slicked down. Daphne placed the diamond and pearl studded tiara on her head and then placed the veil behind it with the tail flowing down her back.

"Okay, turn around and take a look in the mirror," Daphne said, holding the bulk of the dress train that was pinned up on the back of her dress to keep it from getting dirty or wrinkled on the floor of the small room.

"Oh, wow," Bridget said, studying herself in the mirror.

"You're beautiful," Daphne said.

"I agree. You look great, Bridge," Britton said.

"Thanks," Bridget replied, leaning over to hug her best friend and then her sister.

"Oh my," Sharon said, walking back into the room. "You're absolutely beautiful, darling."

"Thanks, mom."

"We need to get dressed," Britton said, pointing to the clock.

"It's crowded in here. You two go down to your room and get ready, Britton," Sharon said.

"Daphne can use one of the spare rooms at the end of the hall," Britton said.

"Your aunt and uncle are in one of the rooms and the groomsmen are in the other at the moment. She can get dressed in your room," Sharon reprimanded.

Britton grabbed her dress and shoes and left the room without looking back. She walked down the hall to her room, laying her dress on the bed and setting the shoes on the floor. Daphne walked in behind her, copying her display.

"Shoot me now," Britton said.

Daphne laughed. "It'll be over soon."

Britton walked closer to her and Daphne threaded her arms around the brunette's neck.

"I'm starting to like being mean to you," Daphne teased.

"Yeah, well, you're pretty good at it. You've had a lot of practice."

"Oh, that's not fair."

Britton pressed her lips to Daphne's, kissing her intensely as her hands ran under her blouse and up the delicate skin of her naked back. Daphne instinctively rocked her hips against Britton's, moaning softly into her mouth. Realizing where they were, both women pulled away, panting and shaking their heads.

"This is going to be a long evening if you get that heated from a tiny touch," Britton said, playfully, leaning in for another quick kiss.

"Shut up," Daphne said, kissing her back. "Go to your side of the room please, or we will never get dressed."

"Fine." Britton grinned, walking around the bed.

They quickly went to work changing into their matching yellow dresses. Daphne turned her back as Britton undressed.

"Really, you're going to get all modest now?" Britton laughed.

"I can't look at you without wanting to touch you," Daphne replied without facing her.

Britton smiled, knowing the feeling was mutual. She finished changing clothes and looked in the mirror.

"How could you let her pick these homely, plain-Jane dresses? I feel like a damn housewife," Britton said.

Daphne laughed, walking over to the same mirror. "Don't blame me. I wasn't involved. Your mother and Bridget went shopping for these."

"Well, at least you could have spoken up when we were at the fitting instead of saying you loved it."

"You didn't exactly say anything either," Daphne chided.

"My opinion didn't count nor matter. I'm the lesbian sister. I have no ground to stand on when it comes to weddings, according to the two of them."

"Uh-huh. What about Heather's bridal party?"

"Those dresses are sensible and sexy. I helped pick them out. We went with something that can be easily worn again. I don't really wear dresses often, but that one will probably get worn again at some point. This thing will be going in my Goodwill pile."

Daphne shook her head. "Come on, Britton-the-homemaker, let's go get this over with."

Chapter Eighteen

The wedding ceremony was beautiful and very heartwarming. Britton felt herself tear up during a few points, but the uncomfortable shoes squeezing and pinching her feet kept her reality in check. The family and wedding party gathered afterwards for the pictures and the photographer seemed to take forever. Britton was glad her father had ordered an open bar because she was going to need a stiff drink when the hour long photo shoot was over.

"I didn't think he would ever finish," Daphne whispered.

"Yeah, me neither. My feet are killing me," Britton whispered back.

They lined up once again to enter the reception tent. The multiple tables full of guests stood, clapping as the wedding party entered and were all seated at a long rectangular table with Bridget and Wade in the center. Daphne was next to Bridget and Britton was next to Daphne with her mother and father beside her. The other side of the table was the same way, with Wade's groomsmen and parents sitting on the end.

Everyone sat down to drink champagne and listen to toast after toast, starting with Stephen Prescott, and then Daphne and Dennis, the maid of honor and best man. They were followed by Wade's father and a few close friends. Britton's feet still ached and she was starving. She'd skipped breakfast and lunch had turned into the hassle of getting her sister dressed, so she never ate all day.

If one more person gets up to make a fucking toast, I'm going to beat them to death with these god damn shoes! she thought.

The food tables were finally opened and the bridal party table was the first to go through the line. Britton skipped the salad, going directly to the pasta and seafood tables. She also swung by the open bar for a vanilla flavored vodka with a splash of cranberry, before going back to the table.

"Hungry?" Daphne laughed.

"I haven't eaten all day," Britton said, digging into the pasta salad that she'd mixed crab and lobster meat into.

"What's that?" Daphne asked, pointing to the pink drink.

"Something to get me through the rest of this evening," Britton grinned.

They were the first two back to the table on their side and no one saw them talking to each other civilly. Daphne snuck a sip of the drink and grimaced.

"Why bother putting cranberry in it at all," Daphne said, frowning.

"Coloring." Britton said, laughing. "I didn't tell you to drink it."

The band finally got the crowd going after all of the tables had been served and staff began picking up the empty plates. They started traditionally with the bride and groom and their parents all dancing together, followed by the wedding party. Britton had to dance with a groomsman named Ricky who pretty much stepped on her feet the entire time. He was also the person she had walked down the aisle with. She was happy to see the dance floor finally open up to everyone.

"Hey, stranger," Heather said.

Britton turned to see her best friend standing behind her. She got up from her seat and hugged her.

"Aren't you a sight for sore eyes," Britton said.

"That bad, huh?"

"You have no idea," Britton said, shaking her head.

"I see you surpassed the champagne and the wine and went straight to the liquor." Heather laughed.

"You would too, trust me."

"Come on, dance with me," Heather said.

Britton walked out to the crowded dance floor, spinning and twisting with her best friend to the fast song that was playing. They smiled, enjoying the music as the song changed to another fast one. Daphne danced nearby, making eye contact with Britton occasionally. Britton smiled at her.

When the music slowed down, Greg walked up to Britton and Heather. "May I have this dance?" he asked Britton.

"Are you sure you don't want to dance with your soon-to-be wife? You guys need the practice," Britton said.

"No. I get to dance with her all day next weekend. Come on. Dancing with me won't make you straight." He laughed.

Britton smacked his arm and went back to the dance floor with him. She'd known him a long time and he often went to her for advice when it came to Heather. She had even been there to help him pick out the ring when he was getting ready to propose.

"I didn't get to thank you for coming to my bachelor party," he said.

"I had a great time. That night that went right on into the next morning." She laughed, remembering the ill-fated dress fitting.

After the dance, Britton wandered around the room talking to various family members and family friends as the evening went on. She danced here and there, but spent most of her time off of the dance floor and off of her aching feet.

Daphne finally found Britton standing off to the side of the room alone. She grabbed another glass of champagne and walked over to her.

"Hey," Britton said. "You better not be seen talking to me," she joked.

"I'll take my chances. I want to talk to you about something," she sighed. "This isn't...maybe I should wait. I don't know."

"Daphne, what the hell are you saying. I can barely hear you and you're talking in riddles," Britton said over the band.

Daphne nodded towards the house. Britton shrugged, following her out of the tent.

"I'm going to my room to change out of these uncomfortable fucking shoes. Come on. We can talk up there," Britton said.

~

Britton walked into her room, sighing as she sat on the bed. She quickly pulled the horrid shoes from her swollen feet.

"Louboutin's, these are not!" Britton said, tossing the shoes on the floor.

Daphne laughed. Agreeing, she adding her shoes to the pile and leaned over, kissing Britton's cheek.

Britton turned her head. Catching Daphne's lips, she kissed her passionately, opening her mouth to taste the champagne on her tongue.

"Don't start something you can't finish," Daphne said, pulling away.

"Who said I can't finish? Besides, I've seen you watching me all night," Britton teased.

Daphne sighed. "I can't get used to wanting you so bad all the time. I can't even look at you without wanting to tear your clothes off."

"How is that a bad thing?" Britton asked, running her hand over Daphne's bare skin above the dress.

Daphne's head sank back as Britton replaced her hand with her mouth.

Dresses were unzipped and tossed to the floor as Britton and Daphne explored each other's body. Britton pulled the bedding back and they moved inside the smooth sheets, kissing and touching like long lost lovers.

Britton rolled onto Daphne, sliding her fingers inside of her as she kissed her passionately. Daphne moaned softly, moving her hips to match the rhythm of Britton's hand as she ran her hands through Britton's hair.

The wedding reception going on below them was long forgotten until a loud scream broke their concentration. Both women turned to see Bridget standing in the doorway with one hand on her chest and the other over her mouth.

Daphne froze and Britton moved off of her.

"Oh my God!" Bridget yelled. "What the hell?!" she yelled again, looking at both women.

"How could you do this?" Bridget screamed at Britton.

"Wait, calm down, Bridget," Britton said.

"Calm down! Are you seriously kidding me?!"

"Bridget, let me explain," Britton said.

"Explain? Explain what? How you coerced my best friend to get in bed with you? Are you drunk, Daphne? What the fuck is going on? And on my wedding day, Britton? How fucking classy is that?" she yelled.

"Bridget, please calm down. It's not what you think," Daphne said.

"Then what is it? Are you drunk? Why are you in bed with my sister? What did she do to you?"

"No, I'm not drunk and your sister didn't force me to do anything. In fact, I initiated it. I'm sorry. I know this is your wedding day," Daphne sighed. "Bridget, I'm a lesbian."

"What the hell are you talking about?" Bridget looked confused.

"I've been a lesbian for a long time. I just didn't know how to tell anyone."

"That doesn't make any sense and even if it's true, how the hell did you wind up in bed with her? You two hate each other!"

Daphne pulled the sheets tightly around herself. "We shared a kiss in high school and it scared me to death. I blamed Britton for it all of these years. I was stupid. I wasted so many years resenting her when really I was attracted to her," she said.

"So, you chose my wedding to have a little fling?!" Bridget yelled.

"It's not a fling, Bridget. I'm in love with her," Daphne said.

Britton's breath caught in her throat and she froze.

Bridget gasped in shock and stormed out of the room. Daphne heard her heels clicking on the hardwood floors and the staircase as she jumped up, trying to get her dress back on.

Daphne put her dress and shoes on quickly and took off out of the room without saying anything. Britton put her dress and shoes back on and rushed out after them.

Bridget walked into the tent clearly upset and Daphne appeared a few seconds later with Britton behind her. Both women looked disheveled.

"What's happened?" Sharon asked, going to Bridget's side as a few people in the room began to notice something was wrong.

"Ask them!" she announced to the entire room.

Everyone turned to see the distressed bride.

"Honey, what's wrong?" Wade asked, running up to her.

"What's going on?" Heather asked, standing near Daphne.

147

"I just made a huge mistake," Daphne said, clearly in shock. "I'm sorry, Bridget," she said, wiping the tears from her eyes.

Britton's heart dropped. "Bridget, Wade, the wedding was beautiful. I wish you both all of the happiness in the world," she said, turning to walk away.

"You ruined everything," Bridget sneered, disappointment weighing heavily on her face.

"I don't understand," Sharon said with her husband coming to her side.

Britton hung her head and sighed. "I'll talk to you both in the morning," she said to her parents, before walking away and leaving Daphne still rooted to the ground in shock.

~

Britton rushed upstairs and changed into the clothes she'd arrived in earlier that day, leaving the dress on the rumpled bed. She never looked back as she got in her car and drove away.

~

Stephen Prescott waved his hand at the band to get them playing again. "Please, everyone have a drink and enjoy yourselves," he said, encouraging the people in the room to continue celebrating.

"I don't understand and right now I don't want to talk about it. Wade, can we please just go," Bridget murmured, wiping her own tears.

"Sure," Wade said, not really knowing what to do.

"Someone needs to explain to me what just happened," Stephen said, stepping back over to his wife and daughter.

"Please, Daddy, can we just say goodbye to everyone?" Bridget said.

Daphne walked out of the tent as Stephen had the band announce that the happy couple was leaving. Everyone gathered to tell them goodbye as Daphne drove away, still wearing her yellow bridesmaid dress.

~

Britton was laying on her couch staring at the blank TV screen when her cell phone rang. She saw the caller ID and decided to answer before he showed up at her door.

"What the hell happened? And where are you?"

"Daddy, I came home. Can I please explain everything tomorrow? I'll come out and have brunch with you and mom."

When he agreed, she hung up and turned her ringer off.

Chapter Nineteen

Britton sat in her car with the top down listening to the waves crash against the cliff below her. Hearing Daphne say she was in love with her was like winning the gold medal she never knew she wanted and then hearing her call everything a mistake a few minutes later was like drowning in the water she'd just won the medal in. Britton wiped the tears from her cheeks. She had single-handedly turned her own life upside-down, managing to ruin her sister's wedding. She'd spent the entire night going over the scenario in her head.

Refusing to drown herself any longer in self-pity, she started the car and turned towards the main road. She needed to begin picking up the pieces of her latest disaster and that started with brunch.

Britton walked into her family home, slightly holding her breath. She wasn't ready for the disappointment she saw in her parent's faces when she found them out on the back patio. An array of food adorned the antique metal-framed table with a glass top.

She sat down, silently praying the orange juice in the decanter was spiked, but knowing her family, it wasn't. Forgoing the juice, she settled on a large cup of coffee and a fresh turkey melt sandwich.

"Bridget and Wade left for Jamaica this morning without saying anything," her father said, setting the newspaper aside. "What the hell happened last night? What did you do to upset your sister so badly?"

Britton sighed. "Bridget caught Daphne and me in bed together."

"Excuse me?" her mother said as if she hadn't heard her correctly.

"Daphne and I were in bed," Britton said, raising her eyebrows and shrugging.

"Oh good lord," her mother blurted.

"It was a mistake. We hadn't meant for that happen," she said, wondering if she could sneak into the house to find something to spike her coffee with. This was like having the layers of her skin peeled back one at a time.

"I can't believe you," Sharon sighed. "And during your sister's wedding...Britton, I can't believe I'm hearing this."

"What do you have to say for yourself?" Stephen asked.

"Daddy, I'm sorry. I never meant to ruin her wedding. It just happened."

"I still don't understand. You and Daphne hate each other. How in the hell did you wind up in bed together? Did you both drink too much?" her mother asked.

"No..." Britton looked at her parents. "We've been seeing each other for a little over a month," she sighed. "When I was fifteen Daphne and I kissed each other. She freaked out and blamed me for everything and has been waiting all of these years for me to tell everyone about it. She's a lesbian, too, but no one here knows. Her family isn't exactly as open as mine. I had no idea the hatred was really an attraction that she was hiding."

"How did all of this come to the surface?" her mother asked.

"We had a huge argument after running into Victoria at Heather's bachelorette party."

"I thought she was out of the picture?" her father said.

"She is and has been. Anyway, she was drunk and at the same bar and she said a bunch of hateful things and it stirred a lot of stuff between Daphne and me. We had a big argument and she finally told me the truth," she said, sipping her coffee.

"I'm still very disappointed in you for doing something like that during your sister's wedding. I thought we raised you better than this, Britton. What happened to having self-respect and respect for others?" her father said.

"I'm really sorry all of this happened the way it did. That was a huge mistake. I don't know what else to say. I'm sure Daphne's parents figured it out. No one knows about her or at least they didn't."

"Thankfully, I believe most of the guests had no clue something was going on," her mother said. "I didn't see her parents leave, though."

"Did Daphne say anything before she left?"

"No. She left right after you did and in the same fashion."

"She's probably going to take this very hard. I wish I could take it all back. It was such a stupid mistake," Britton said, wiping a lone tear before it fell.

"Are you in love with Daphne?" her mother asked.

Britton looked at mother with a perplexed expression. Her parents knew she was gay and had never questioned her about her lifestyle and her mother had never showed much interest in that side of her life. She thought for a moment, taking a bite of her untouched sandwich.

Seeing the confusion on her daughter's face, Sharon said, "I just want to know if there will be another wedding in the near future."

Britton's eyes practically bugged out of her head. She coughed up the piece of sandwich she'd practically swallowed whole. Regaining her composure, Britton stared at her mother and looked to her father for a little assistance, but he stayed mute.

"That's the last thing on my mind. We've only been seeing each other a month and I wouldn't even call it dating. She doesn't even live in the same state and no one could see us out together here, so we were sneaking around. I don't even know what to call it," Britton said.

Sharon shook her head at her daughter. "Are you in love with her or not?"

"Yes," Britton finally said, feeling deflated.

"That's good because if you ruined your sister's wedding for a fling, I was going to choke you myself," her mother said with a serious tone in her voice. "Now, go to that girl and tell her because if you let a woman like Daphne get away I will personally cut you off."

Britton stiffened. She'd never seen this side of her mother and it shocked and scared her. She looked at her dad again.

He shrugged. "I'd listen to her if I were you," he said.

Britton left without another word. She was still in shock as she drove across the bay towards New Bedford. She wasn't sure what to say and hadn't planned anything out. She was still trying to sort out all of the craziness of the past twenty hours as she turned into the driveway, parking behind Daphne's car.

Britton knocked softly. Daphne pulled the door open with her brows creased in surprise. She tried to smile, but couldn't get past a half-hearted grin. Britton walked inside, pulling Daphne into her arms. Daphne sank into her, sighing deeply.

"How are you doing?" Britton asked.

Daphne pulled away from her, searching gray eyes. "I just spent the morning on the phone with my mother, trying to explain why I was caught having sex with my best friend's sister during her wedding reception where I was the maid of honor! How do you think I feel?!" she snapped.

"I'm sorry," Britton said.

"It didn't help matters when you left me standing there alone to face everyone."

Britton hung her head. "I heard you say you made a huge mistake. That stung more than everything else combined."

Daphne stepped closer. "Britton, I did make a huge mistake. We should never have gone upstairs together. I don't for a second regret being with you."

"Did you mean what you said?" Britton asked.

Daphne's face wrinkled with confusion. She waited for Britton to continue.

"You told Bridget you were in love with me," Britton said, just above a whisper.

Daphne smiled. Wrapping her arms around Britton, she pulled her close. "Yes. I've been in love with you for years. I finally admitted it to myself," she said, kissing Britton softly.

Britton leaned back slightly, sighing with relief.

"What was that for?" Daphne asked, raising an eyebrow.

"I spent the morning having breakfast with my parents."

"Yikes," Daphne said.

"It wasn't too bad actually. After they scolded me like a child for my behavior yesterday, my mother threatened to cut off my inheritance if I let you get away," Britton said, seriously.

Daphne laughed.

"I'm not kidding!" she said.

"I see. So, it's about the money," Daphne teased.

"No, she's just started planning our wedding already," Britton said, honestly.

Daphne backed away with a stunned expression on her face.

Britton grinned and Daphne smiled at her.

"I love the way you smile at me," Britton said, moving closer. "I love the way we fit together," she said, wrapping her arms around Daphne's waist. "And I love you," she finished, kissing her intensely.

Daphne ran her hands up Britton's chest, laying her palms above her breasts and returning the kiss feverishly, before pushing Britton back to the couch. Britton flopped down on her back and Daphne crawled on top of her, holding Britton's hands above her head. She wiggled her eyebrows and grinned as she leaned down, claiming Britton's lips and continuing the passionate kiss.

Chapter Twenty

Britton was happy to see Monday coming to a close. She was tired from the crazy weekend and was really looking forward to meeting Heather for a drink after work. She still hadn't told her what happened, although anyone that saw the situation had a pretty good idea what was going on.

Britton took a seat at the open bar, ordering two glasses of merlot as she looked around for her friend. Surprisingly, Britton wasn't running late and had arrived at the wine bar with a few minutes to spare. She ran a hand through her thick hair, pushing it over her shoulder. She couldn't believe how quickly and dramatically her life had changed in the last six weeks. She kept waiting for someone to shake her awake.

"Hey," Heather said, bringing her back to reality as she slid onto the stool next to her.

"Hey yourself. I ordered for you," Britton said as the bartender set the glass down in front of Heather.

"Oh, you're a godsend," she said, taking a long swallow.

"Rough day?" Britton asked.

"Work was fine. My step-monster on the other hand is driving me crazy. The wedding is in a few days and she's trying to add some people to the guest list. Apparently, they are new friends of her and my father. My mom is pissed and I'm stuck in the middle."

"That's crazy. What did your father say?"

"I haven't talked to him. He worships the ground that bitch walks on. I'm sure he will just tell me to add them in. I guess they will be sitting on the floor because we have exactly enough seats at the reception. At this point, I really don't give a shit anymore. I told you we should have eloped," Heather said, shaking her head.

"It sounds like you have a lot more on your plate than I do," Britton smiled. "I got the permits today for my father's building so we are set to break ground a week from Monday."

"That's great. I bet he's happy."

"Yeah, I talked to his assistant, but I'm sure Dad's ready to get it going."

"Quit beating around the bush and spill it," Heather said, staring at her best friend.

"Spill what?"

"You know what." Heather raised an eyebrow, waiting patiently.

"Oh, I thought maybe you'd forgotten all about that," Britton bit her bottom lip, avoiding eye contact.

"Did you really have sex during your sister's wedding reception? And with Daphne, of all people?" Heather asked.

"Something like that."

"Were you drunk?"

Britton sighed heavily. "No. We've been seeing each other for a little over a month."

"What?!" Heather yelped.

Britton stared at her.

"No shit?!" Heather asked.

"No shit." Britton answered.

"Wow," she said, shaking her head. "How the hell did that happen?"

"We ran into each other at the Prescott building right after your bachelorette party. She was there when I presented the new building model to the company and we talked. I guess I should go back to the beginning," Britton said, pausing to order another glass of wine.

"Do you remember our sophomore year of high school? You and I used to go practice rowing all the time." Britton continued.

"Yeah."

"Well, we finished rowing one Saturday afternoon and I went home afterwards to find Daphne naked in my bathroom. She had just finished using my shower, which apparently Bridget said was okay to do since I wasn't home. Anyway, I didn't know she was in there and I walked in through my room, stripping off my shirt and sports bra. She was walking out at the same time and we saw each other. She started to scream, but stopped when her eyes saw my naked chest. We shared a very heated, passionate kiss before Bridget called for her down the hall."

"Holy shit!"

"She apparently blamed me for the whole thing and was scared I was going to tell everyone. That's why she has treated me like shit for so long."

"It's starting to make sense now," Heather said, sipping her second glass of wine. "But, how did you wind up in bed together in the first place? I thought she was straight."

"No, she's a lesbian as much as I am, trust me," Britton grinned. "She just didn't know how to tell her family."

Heather shook her head in shock. "I don't know what to say," she paused. "Wait, have you two been sneaking around this entire time?"

"Yeah, something like that," Britton said, sheepishly.

"Britton, you dog. Why didn't you at least tell me? I'm your best friend."

"I don't know. It just happened and at first I thought it was going to be a one-time thing, but it was too damn good to stop," she said, grinning.

Heather laughed.

"I think I'm still floored," Heather said, shaking her head. "Okay, so how did you wind up screwing during the reception?"

Britton laughed. "I went upstairs to change out of those god-awful shoes and she came with me. One thing led to another and the next thing I know we're going at it and my sister is screaming like a banshee in the doorway."

"Oh God."

"It was a huge mistake. I feel really bad about it. Neither of us ever meant for that to happen. Bridget left on her honeymoon still pissed at me, Daphne had to come out to her parents, and I got scolded like a child by mine. Oh and my mom wants me to marry Daphne."

Heather laughed.

"I'm serious," Britton said.

"Wow. What did you say?"

"I didn't. I left," Britton said, laughing.

"Does your mother know you don't want to get married?"

"I guess she's going to find out." Britton shrugged.

"What a crazy weekend."

"Yeah, you're telling me," Britton said.

"How did my aunt and uncle take Daphne's coming out? I saw them at the wedding and spoke to them briefly before all of the commotion."

"Your aunt was really hard on her. She hasn't said much about it."

"Yeah, her mother pretends to go to church and be a saint. It drives my mom nuts." Heather said, sighing. "Why don't we all get together Wednesday night? The three of us."

"That sounds good."

"I'll call Daphne later. Does she know you're here with me?"

"No. I haven't talked to her since I left her place this morning."

"So, it's pretty serious?" Heather asked.

"I'm in love with her," Britton said.

"Wow. Is the sex really that good?" Heather teased.

Britton smiled brightly. "Even better," she said.

"Huh, my cousin Daphne, the lesbian love goddess. Who knew?" Heather said, mockingly.

Britton laughed.

~

Wednesday night rolled around quickly. Britton walked into the restaurant to find her lover and her best friend sitting at a corner table, sipping wine and waiting for the notoriously late to arrive.

"It's about time you showed up," Heather sneered, smiling. "We better stop talking about her," she said to Daphne.

"Yeah, we wouldn't want to inflate that ego any larger," Daphne added.

"Oh nice, did you two get together and decide to gang up on me tonight?" Britton asked.

"No, we love you, so it's all in good fun. At your expense, of course." Daphne grinned.

"I see." Britton nodded. "So, have the nerves kicked in yet? Three days to go," she said to Heather.

"No. I told you. I'm not going to be nuts like your sister. It's been a long time coming and I'm honestly ready to get it over with before I murder some family members."

"Your parents are much better than mine, even if they are somewhat twisted," Daphne said. "My dad has barely spoken to me and my mom is still in shock. She's probably said a hundred Hail Mary's and pretended to go to church three times already and it's only Wednesday."

Heather laughed. "I'm sorry. I know it's not funny. On a good note, my mother is thrilled that you two hooked up. She said she will gladly adopt you if you want."

Daphne smiled. "Aww, I love Aunt Claire. Your mom is definitely the opposite of mine. How the hell did two sisters grow up to be so completely different?"

"I have no idea," Heather said.

"Look at me and Bridget. We're like day and night. Hell, we don't even look alike. I'm glad I look like my dad, otherwise I was beginning to wonder if I was the milkman's kid," Britton said.

"Yeah, you and your sister definitely look like your parents and not each other. That's a good thing though. I have never been attracted to Bridget. Not at all, but you," she paused, shaking her head. "I couldn't stand to be around you when I was a teenager because my body went nuts on its own," Daphne said.

"Wow, you had it bad for her all this time?" Heather asked.

"Yeah. And to top it off, I thought you two were together," Daphne said.

"What made you think that?"

"You two were inseparable. Hell, you still are. Everyone knew Britton was a lesbian, so I assumed you were together."

Heather laughed. "I wonder how many people thought that?"

"I don't know. I guess we will find out at our reunion one day," Britton said.

"You should have said something, Daphne. That would've saved us all from years of turmoil," Heather said.

"Trust me, I know."

"Seriously, I'm glad you two finally figured things out. Don't worry about what anyone says. You look good together and I don't think I've ever seen you this happy, Britton."

"Thanks," Britton said.

"Just promise me you won't fornicate at my reception," Heather teased.

Graysen Morgen

"Nah, we were thinking we'd get it on during your wedding, maybe sneak behind the pulpit. Sex in a church could be really hot," Britton said.

"We'd definitely be going to hell," Daphne said, laughing.

"Oh please. I'm driving the bus to hell, everyone get on!" Britton joked.

164

Chapter Twenty-One

Britton and Daphne arrived at the church together after spending Friday night rolling around the sheets of Britton's bed. They were tired, but excited to share Heather's special day with her.

"You two both look like that cat that ate the canary," Heather's mom said, seeing them walk in together.

Britton laughed and Daphne looked nervous.

"I'm happy for you. You know you're both like daughters to me," she said.

"Thanks Aunt Claire," Daphne said, hugging her aunt.

"You don't worry about your mom. I had a little talk with her. I think she's going to come around, eventually," she said, smiling at her niece. "Now, you both better get in there and get that bride ready. I have to go sharpen my claws. The bitch will be here soon," she grinned, walking away.

Britton laughed hysterically.

165

"Wow. I never realized it was that tense after the divorce," Daphne said.

Britton grabbed her hand, pulling her down the hallway. She grinned, taking in the paintings and crosses on the walls in the belly of the church as she squeezed Daphne's hand tighter. "You have no idea. We were the big scene at Bridget's wedding, but those two may snatch each other bald at this one."

Daphne laughed, shaking her head.

"It's about time you two got here," Heather growled.

"Whoa, calm down. I thought you weren't going to be a bridezilla today?" Britton reminded her.

"I know. I'm sorry. My mom won't stop talking about Marianne. I'm ready to knock her out," Heather said.

"I know what will help her. Daphne, can you get things started here? I'll be back in a few minutes."

"Okay?" Daphne said, curiously.

Britton grinned, kissing her lips softly, before leaving the room.

"What's she going to do?" Heather asked.

"Probably go buy them some boxing gloves or something," Daphne said, seriously, as she began arranging the dress, pantyhose, shoes, veil, and corset in the order they would go on.

"Your hair and makeup look great. Britton told me your mom took you to the salon this morning," she said, looking back at Heather who was standing behind her, laughing. "What?" Daphne asked.

"You and Britton belong together," she said, shaking her head.

Daphne smiled. "Come on, this shit takes forever to get on."

Britton returned to the church a few minutes later with two bottles of wine and four glasses. She went in search of Heather's mom, finding her sitting in a pew, filing her freshly painted fingernails.

She wasn't kidding, Britton thought, walking up to her.

"Claire, I got something for you. Come back to Heather's dressing room," she grinned, pulling one of the bottles slightly out of the bag.

Claire smiled and nodded.

Britton walked into the room to see Daphne helping Heather with her pantyhose.

"Oh, this is a nice sight," she teased.

"Go to hell," Heather said, laughing.

"I'm driving the bus to hell! Remember?!" Britton said. "You're lucky you have her helping you. I have no idea how to get those things on."

"She's not very good at getting them off either," Daphne whispered.

Heather laughed.

"I heard that," Britton said, removing the bottles and glasses from the bag.

"Oh my God, you really are going to hell now." Heather giggled.

"Hello ladies, I was told you needed some assistance," Claire said, entering the room.

Britton poured the four glasses and passed them around, before helping Heather get ready.

~

Two hours later, Daphne and Britton had finished getting Heather ready and were putting on their own dresses. Britton stripped from her jeans and shirt, revealing her athletically toned body. Daphne paused in the middle of pulling her dress up to watch her, as did Heather. Claire had left the room once she had a good buzz going.

"You kill me. I don't know how the hell you still have a knockout body," Heather said.

Britton shrugged. "Once an athlete, always an athlete, I guess. My metabolism is still really high and I go to the gym when I can."

"When's the last time you went rowing?" Daphne asked.

"I haven't rowed since I graduated high school. I was too busy in college and then I graduated and started working," Britton said, pulling her dress on.

"I tried to teach Greg, but he just about drowned me. He has no balance whatsoever," Heather said. "What about you, Daphne. Do you still row?"

"No. Not since high school, either."

"You two look great," Heather said, eyeing their dresses.

"I love these shoes," Daphne said, pulling the straps over her feet.

"I'm just glad they're comfortable," Britton said.

A knock on the door drew their attention.

Leslie walked into the room, already dressed in her bridesmaid dress and shoes. Everyone smiled politely.

"The guests are starting to arrive," Leslie said.

Britton checked the clock on the wall. "We have about a half hour before this shindig kicks off," she said. "Leslie, would you like a glass of wine?"

"No, thanks," Leslie said, looking at her oddly.

Britton turned to Daphne and rolled her eyes.

~

The wedding ceremony was more religious than Britton would have liked, but it was beautiful. She couldn't be happier for her best friend. As soon as the bride and groom walked down the aisle, they left in an old Rolls Royce limo with the rest of the wedding party riding behind them in another white limo. The guests filed out of the church one row at a time, heading to their cars to drive over to the reception at the Grand Hotel up the street.

When the church was all cleared out, the two limos circled back around. The wedding party went back into the church for an hour-long photo shoot. Britton and Daphne gathered all of their stuff and Heather's from the bridal room and drove Britton's car to the hotel when they were finished with their portion of the photos. They had a rented room for the night and hurried upstairs to put everything away and steal a few long, passionate kisses before going back downstairs in time for the arrival of the bridal party in the limos.

The reception room was beautifully decorated in white and silver with many large round tables full of guests. The bridal party was at a long rectangular table in the front near the dance floor with everyone situated similar to the way Bridget's reception had been, except the parents were not at the main table.

Heather's father opened the reception with a toast and Britton stood up after him.

"I remember when we were five years old, twenty years ago for those that don't know that," she paused. "Heather was sitting alone, playing in the sand. I sat down next to her and she asked me to be her friend. Who knew that would lead to a lifetime of friendship, so long ago," she paused again, smiling at Heather. "A few short years later, we were sitting on the floor in her room playing with her Barbie dolls making Barbie and Ken have a wedding. Heather looked at me and asked if I would be her maid," Britton giggled. "Of course I said yes."

Everyone in the room laughed.

"Back then, we had no idea why the people in the weddings were called maids, we just assumed that's how things were," She paused again, smiling at Heather. "Here we are twenty years later and I'm still your best friend and today, I was so very proud and honored to be your maid," she said, smiling and wiping away a few tears. "I love you, Heather and I couldn't be happier for you. Greg, you had better be good to her," she said turning towards the crowd. "Here's to a lifetime of happiness for Heather and Greg."

Everyone cheered and Heather wrapped her arms around Britton when she sat down.

"That was beautiful. I'm glad I chose you to be my friend and my maid." Heather laughed.

A few more people gave toasts before the food was served and the full cash bar opened up. The DJ called for the bride and groom to have their first dance, followed by the wedding party and then the family of the bride and groom. As soon as the dance floor opened to everyone, Britton mingled around the room talking to a few friends and other table guests before stopping at her parent's table.

"That's a cute speech you gave, darling," Britton's mother said.

"Thanks, Mom."

"Do you feel like cutting the rug, Daddy?" Britton asked.

"Well, you didn't dance with me at your sister's wedding, so I figured you didn't want to be seen dancing with your old man," he said.

She had hoped no one would bring up Bridget's wedding, especially since she and Wade were sitting at the same table as her parents. "My feet were killing me in those shoes. I was lucky to get through the bridal party dance," she said, holding her hand out to her father.

Stephen Prescott stood, buttoning his jacket, before taking his daughter's hand and walking to the center of the dance floor. They shared a semi-fast dance and then a slower song came on. Britton couldn't remember the last time she'd danced in her father's arms, but he felt so strong next to her, making her feel like a little girl again. When the song was over, she kissed his cheek and thanked him.

"That was really sweet," Daphne said, bumping arms with her near the bar.

"I don't think he will ever get over the disappointment, but he's starting to come around a little bit at a time."

"I could never find a reason to be disappointed in you. You're a brilliantly talented artist. He will see that one day."

"Thanks," Britton leaned over, kissing her cheek softly. "I love you," she whispered.

"I love you, too," Daphne said.

"Hey now, knock that touchy-feely stuff off," Heather teased, wrapping her arms around them both.

"I just spoke to my parents," Daphne said.

"Oh really? How did that go? I avoided their table like the plague," Britton replied.

"They don't understand, but my mom did say she wanted to see me happy. So, I guess it's a start." Daphne smiled thinly.

"They will come around. My mom will make sure of it," Heather smiled, before walking away to talk to more of her guests.

Britton wrapped her arm around Daphne's waist, squeezing her close, before turning to walk away.

"Do you have a minute?" Bridget asked, walking up to Britton and Daphne.

They both nodded.

"I'm still in shock, I won't lie to you. None of this makes any sense to me," she said.

"Bridget, I'm so sorry. I never meant for you to find out that way and I'm appalled at my own behavior at your wedding," Daphne said.

"I'm sorry, too, Bridge. We made a huge mistake," Britton said.

"I'm actually glad the two of you finally figured things out between you," she said, shaking her head. "If anything, I thought I would find you scratching each other's eyes out."

Britton laughed.

"How was Jamaica?" Daphne asked.

"Hot! I'm glad we decided to only go for six days. That was plenty long enough for the both of us," Bridget exclaimed. "I'm not looking forward to going back to work, but I am glad to be home."

"That's good. I'm glad you guys had a good time," Britton added.

"Take care of each other," Bridget said, seriously, before hugging them both and walking away.

"Dance with me," Britton said, turning to face Daphne.

"Really?"

"Why not?" Britton shrugged.

Daphne grinned and walked out to the dance floor with Britton behind her. They wrapped their arms around each other, careful not to get too close as they swayed to the slow song, oblivious to the numerous stares from around the room. A few people walked off the dance floor but Heather and Greg joined them, followed by Bridget and Wade and Britton and Bridget's parents. Heather's mother and stepfather also appeared on the dance floor.

Daphne noticed everyone around them, smiling at the dancing pair. She pulled Britton tighter, exhaling the breath that she'd been holding.

~

The reception started to wind down after the cake was cut and served. Britton was tired from dancing and glad that she and Daphne had booked a room for the night. She laughed, watching Greg remove the garter from Heather's leg and toss it into the crowd of single men.

The DJ called for the single women to enter the dance floor for the bride to throw the bouquet. Britton walked to the edge of the group, not really paying attention as the music began. Heather turned, smiling at the ladies, before turning her back to them and tossing the flowers over her head. The women in the center of the circle jumped, but the flowers floated further back, landing silently into Daphne's hands.

Sharon Prescott cheered loudly with excitement from the edge of the floor where she was standing with her husband and other guests, watching the toss.

"Noooo!" Britton shrieked.

About the Author

Graysen Morgen is the bestselling author of *Falling Snow* and *Fast Pitch*, as well as many other titles. She was born and raised in North Florida with winding rivers and waterways at her back door and the white sandy beach a mile away. She has spent most of her lifetime in the sun and on the water. She enjoys reading, writing, fishing, and spending as much time as possible with her partner and their daughter.

You can contact Graysen at graysenmorgen@aol.com and like her fan page on facebook.com/graysenmorgen.

Go to www.tri-pub.com to get information about Triplicity Publishing or to submit your manuscript.

Other Titles Available From

Triplicity Publishing

Falling Snow by Graysen Morgen. Dr. Cason Macauley, a high-speed trauma surgeon from Denver meets Adler Troy, a professional snowboarder and sparks fly. The last thing Cason wants is a relationship and Adler doesn't realize what's right in front of her until it's gone, but will it be too late?

Fate vs. Destiny by Graysen Morgen. Logan Greer devotes her life to investigating plane crashes for the National Transportation Safety Board. Brooke McCabe is an investigator with the Federal Aviation Association who literally flies by the seat of her pants. When Logan gets tangled in head games with both women will she choose fate or destiny?

Just Me by Graysen Morgen. Wild child Ian Wiley has to grow up and take the reins of the hundred year old family business when tragedy strikes. Cassidy Harland is a little surprised that she came within an inch of picking up a gorgeous stranger in a bar and is shocked to find out that stranger is the new head of her company.

Love Loss Revenge by Graysen Morgen. Rian Casey is an FBI Agent working the biggest case of her career and madly in love with her girlfriend. Her world is turned upside when tragedy strikes. Heartbroken, she tries to rebuild her life. When she discovers the truth behind what really happened that awful night she decides justice isn't good enough, and vows revenge on everyone involved.

Natural Instinct by Graysen Morgen. Chandler Scott is a Marine Biologist who keeps her private life private. Corey Joslen is intrigued by Chandler from the moment she meets her. Chandler is forced to finally open her life up to Corey. It backfires in Corey's face and sends her running. Will either woman learn to trust her natural instinct?

Secluded Heart by Graysen Morgen. Chase Leery is an overworked cardiac surgeon with a group of best friends that have an opinion and a reason for everything. When she meets a new artist named Remy Sheridan at her best friend's art gallery she is captivated by the reclusive woman. When Chase finds out why Remy is so sheltered will she put her career on the line to help her or is it too difficult to love someone with a secluded heart?

In Love, at War by Graysen Morgen. Charley Hayes is in the Army Air Force and stationed at Ford Island in Pearl Harbor. She is the commanding officer of her own female-only service squadron and doing the one thing she loves most, repairing airplanes. Life is good for Charley, until the day she finds herself falling in love while fighting for her life as her country

Graysen Morgen

is thrown haphazardly into World War II. Can she survive being in love and at war?

Fast Pitch by Graysen Morgen. Graham Cahill is a senior in college and the catcher and captain of the softball team. Despite being an all-star pitcher, Bailey Michaels is young and arrogant. Graham and Bailey are forced to get to know each other off the field in order to learn to work together on the field. Will the extra time pay off or will it drive a nail through the team?

Submerged by Graysen Morgen. Assistant District Attorney Layne Carmichael had no idea that the sexy woman she took home from a local bar for a one night stand would turn out to be someone she would be prosecuting months later. Scooter is a Naval Officer on a submarine who changes women like she changes uniforms. When she is accused of a heinous crime she is shocked to see her latest conquest sitting across from her as the prosecuting attorney.

Vow of Solitude by Austen Thorne. Detective Jordan Denali is in a fight for her life against the ghosts from her past and a Serial Killer taunting her with his every move. She lives a life of solitude and plans to keep it that way. When Callie Marceau, a curious Medical Examiner, decides she wants in on the biggest case of her career, as well as, Jordan's life, Jordan is powerless to stop her.

Igniting Temptation by Sydney Canyon. Mackenzie Trotter is the Head of Pediatrics at the local hospital. Her life takes a rather unexpected turn when she meets a flirtatious, beautiful fire fighter. Both women soon discover it doesn't take much to ignite temptation.

One Night by Sydney Canyon. While on a business trip, Caylen Jarrett spends an amazing night with a beautiful stripper. Months later, she is shocked and confused when that same woman re-enters her life. The fact that this stranger could destroy her career doesn't bother her. C.J. is more terrified of the feelings this woman stirs in her. Could she have fallen in love in one night and not even known it?

CPSIA information can be obtained at www.ICGtesting.com
Printed in the USA
LVOW05s1226070414

380649LV00052B/1007/P